AN EXILE'S PERFECT LETTER

LARRY MATHEWS

Breakwater Books
P.O. Box 2188, St. John's, NL, Canada, A1C 6E6
www.breakwaterbooks.com

Copyright © 2018 Larry Mathews
ISBN 978-1-55081-707-2

A CIP catalogue record for this book is available from
Library and Archives Canada.

We acknowledge the support of the Canada Council for
the Arts, which last year invested $153 million to bring the
arts to Canadians throughout the country. We acknowledge
the financial support of the Government of Canada and the
Government of Newfoundland and Labrador through the
Department of Tourism, Culture, Industry and Innovation
for our publishing activities.

Printed and bound in Canada.

Breakwater Books is committed to choosing papers
and materials for our books that help to protect our
environment. To this end, this book is printed on a recycled
paper that is certified by the Forest Stewardship Council®.

Canada Council   Conseil des Arts
for the Arts   du Canada

Newfoundland
Labrador

Canadä

RECYCLED
Paper made from
recycled material
FSC   FSC® C103567
www.fsc.org

For Tim and Sal

all this
so one might send an exile's perfect letter
to an ancient hometown friend

—Leonard Cohen

ONE

think I may be in love with my dentist.

This thought crosses my mind as I stare into the eyes of Dr. Sherry Kirsch, on the occasion of my first visit to her practice. Dr. Kirsch—or Sherry, as I've already begun to think of her—seems to have violet eyes, or maybe it's a trick of the light. Does anyone really have violet eyes? Can't be contacts, since she's wearing glasses. Or perhaps the glasses are props, placebos designed to give patients the sense that one is dealing with, being dealt with by, a serious professional and not merely some bimbo who's managed to scrape through dentistry school on the basis of charm alone.

She's what you might call "petite"—or would if you were still in the 1950s—and there's a sweet earnestness about her nearly pretty face as she gives me the scoop on what's happening inside my mouth. Why only "nearly pretty," and what does that even mean? Strike that from the record. We're not judging here. There's something, not to put too fine a point on it, *sexy* about the brisk professionalism of her manner that trumps any pointless detailing of physical features (perfectly disciplined shortish dark hair, but no opportunity to observe the contours of her body, concealed as it is beneath her dentist's scrubs). And as for what's happening inside my mouth—not much, is apparently the bottom line, but the subtext is that it's *me* she's telling me about, there's no reason to change anything in the immediate future, I'm okay, I will continue to be okay, I've received the blessing of the secular priestess, she who knows everything it is necessary to know.

There is of course that mysterious fracture in the upper left incisor, of which I have until now been unaware.

"What could have caused it?" I ask her, eager to show I'm no passive recipient of her wisdom but a keen, self-motivated student of all things dental. Why wouldn't I have noticed when it happened?

"Who knows," she says. "It's probably something that happened eons ago."

"Like so much else in my life," I reply, with what I hope seems like rueful, self-deprecating wit.

I'm sixty-two. Sherry can't be much over thirty.

She smiles. Her teeth are perfect.

I have sought out the services of Dr. Sherry Kirsch, DDS, because my last dentist, Dr. Sylvester O'Connor, committed suicide a few months back. An occupational hazard of dentists, conventional wisdom has it. Theories abound. At his funeral, attended by a strong representation of his clientele (not me, though), it was noted that neither his wife nor his daughter expressed much in the way of grief, both having been seen to sport tight, self-satisfied little smiles. The only public blubbering emanated from his long-time receptionist, unlikely to have been an erotic interest of his, but sounding sincere nonetheless. And where, people said sympathetically, would she get another job at her age?

Sylvester was seventy.

This being St. John's, there was a literary angle. A character based on Sylvester figured prominently in a story by a local writer published, remarkably, in *Harper's* around 1980. He was the cheating husband in a love triangle. The story was widely anthologized, but the writer never published another. She too is dead.

Sylvester's daughter would have been born around the time the story was published, though who knows what significance, if any, that fact might have. But as a card-carrying English prof, I have to think there might be one, even if I don't really want to "uncover" or "unearth" it.

So here I am in Sherry's chair, sitting up with what I hope is a reasonably dignified posture as she browses through the material in the envelope I've retrieved from Sylvester's office. The examination was over quickly. She began by feeling my neck, something Sylvester certainly never did, but which, she explained, was standard procedure for her (lest, presumably, I should conclude that there's something special about *my* neck).

Oh, and Sherry, those ridiculous gloves, you don't need them, not with me of all patients. You have nothing to fear, truly. Shed them. Shed them.

My exercise in mind control having failed, I listened, fascinated, as she told the story of each of my teeth in turn to her bored but attentive hygienist amanuensis. Buckle here, crown there, this that and the other thing somewhere else, fifty-percent overbite. Sherry! Isn't that a bit harsh. Can't we shade the truth a little here? Or perhaps, for all I know, a fifty-percent overbite is as good as it gets, some sort of golden mean, a phenomenon any dentist is glad to discover.

Now she's looking at the information sheet I filled out earlier. I've answered No to all the questions aimed at finding something wrong with me. "No medication?" She looks skeptical. "Of any kind?"

No. Nothing.

"Vitamin supplements?"

No. Go ahead. Keep asking, Sherry. You know you want to. But she doesn't.

Perhaps she intuits the truth.

Yes, there on a shelf above her computer is a photo of her, a man, and two young children, but who knows what that may mean? Nothing conclusive certainly, a PR gesture, reassuring image of domestic normality. For all I know the diploma on the wall of the outer office is bogus too. But what odds.

"Lots of work down the road," Sherry is saying. "But nothing immediate. And I think the university plan covers major."

It doesn't, I know, but I don't want to contradict her.

"Wouldn't want to hit you with a thousand dollars out of the blue...."

Sherry! What's a thousand? Don't even think about it. I'll give it to you right now.

She's slender under her light blue coverall, her dark hair appropriately under stringent control, only a single ringlet dangling free.

Sherry Kirsch. What were your parents thinking? It would be nice if people associated our daughter with the idea of a sweet alcoholic haze? If she turns out to have a drinking problem, people won't be judgmental—they'll say, With a name like that, what can you expect?

And where are you from? Not here, either by name or accent. Your husband (maybe ex- by now) is probably a Newfoundlander. You met him at dentistry school on the mainland. Refused to change your name. Good self-assertive gesture. But then he insisted you both move here, and you caved. Not so good. Or is it: willing to compromise, willing to try new things. That'd be okay, then.

She leads me back to the outer office, where the receptionist tells her the university won't pay for major.

Am I afraid to visit the dentist was a question on the sheet I filled out. Actually I'd prefer, just now, not to leave the place where Sherry is. Not, of course, that I'm afraid, exactly.

She's "happy" about the condition of my gums, she's said. Happy.

Of course I'm not really in love with my dentist. That particular cloud-capped tower comes tumbling down the instant I step into the parking lot of the strip mall where Sherry's, Dr. Kirsch's, office is located.

There's the hot sun, the banality of asphalt, the rows of motionless vehicles somehow radiating an aura of stolid insolence, as though having ignored the commands of their owners to take them somewhere. There's also the dispiriting insight that with all the resources of the human imagination hypothetically at their disposal, the folks who control this parcel of land could think no higher thought than: Parking.

But it's not only that.

There, heaving herself out of what appears to be an absurdly undersized Yaris, is my colleague, Dr. Bernadette O'Keefe. She seems to be shaking her generously proportioned clouds of gray hair *at* me, though I can't quite believe this. "Hugh," she says, mock-severely but with a layer of real severity tucked away in there somewhere. "We need to talk."

"Uh, do we?"

"Don't be coy, Hugh. You know what I mean. Does the phrase *ludic narrative* ring a bell?"

"Tolls me right on back to my sole self," I say, never at a loss for creaky pedantic jollity.

Bernadette's brief smile is suggestive of someone tasting an obscure wine and quickly deciding No thank you.

She has what I imagine would in other circumstances be the aura of the Mother Superior about her, something that strongly implies (without stating anything directly, mind) that one should pay attention. Or, possibly, else. My colleague Barney Power loves to tell the story of being approached by a student looking for Bernadette, but unable to remember her name. "You know, sir," the student said, "the one that looks like a grandmother hippie." Barney, not a fan of Bernadette, is so pleased with this anecdote that he repeats it two or three times a year, making sure Bernadette is out of earshot.

"Here for my physio," she says, waggling her cane as if to evoke the unmentionable complexity of her constellation of ailments.

Beothuk Physio occupies the same building as the Colonial Dental Centre.

"Teeth," I explain.

"Hugh, about that proposal…"

Bernadette and I are members of the departmental graduate studies committee, responsible for, among much else, approving thesis proposals. She has a bee in her bonnet about

"Destabilizing Indeterminacy: A Poststructural Analysis of Three Ludic Narratives," submitted by a student unknown to either of us, to be supervised by our newest young hotshot, Lister Craddock, noted mainly for his ironic T-shirts and general sense of entitlement.

"Surely you must agree," Bernadette is saying. "Not a single English-language-written work."

"How many hyphens would you put in there?"

"What?"

"I'd put in two. Between *English* and *language*, of course, but also, and here's where it gets dicey, between *language* and *written*. What do you think?"

"Don't try to change the subject, Hugh. This is serious."

"But so are hyphens. Why don't people use them anymore?"

Bernadette doesn't respond to this question, but reminds me that the student plans to write about a novel translated from Spanish (whose title I've already forgotten), a Chinese film (ditto), and a video game titled something like *Major Felony Gangsta*. Bernadette doesn't understand how a video game can be regarded as a "narrative," ludic or otherwise. But the student asserts that all three "texts," as she calls them, will be shown to be ideal vehicles for the exploration of the world of ludic narrativity, said world having been discovered by a couple of no-name theorists in whose ground-breaking footsteps she will be pleased to follow. This is what passes for significant novelty in these parts, though really the project promises to be a hunting-and-gathering exercise, which will nevertheless pass easily, if recent history is any guide.

But not if Bernadette can help it.

"Need to take a stand on this one," she's saying. "Are we now the Department of Everything *but* English Literature? Or, well, not just *English* Literature, but you know what I mean."

She has me pegged for an ally. We both teach Creative Writing (me, fiction; she, poetry). We both publish in unpopular areas (me, on obscure Canadian fiction writers; she, poetry). That is, she publishes poetry itself, not articles *about* poetry. Her most recent book, *Rampsing along the Landwash*, was widely praised on the mainland for its attempt to preserve authentic Newfoundland speech (though "widely," as applied to a volume of poetry, is of course intrinsically hyperbolic). And precisely what the mainland reviewers knew about authentic Newfoundland speech was somewhat unclear. Perhaps they were relying on the author's preface, which stated that "where possible, every noun, verb, adjective, and adverb is taken from *The Dictionary of Newfoundland English*." Only one commentator slyly noted "a certain gimmicky quality." The book was nominated for a major award, which fact Bernadette took as supreme validation of her literary career, despite her contempt, in other contexts, for "the mainland literary establishment."

In any case, she's long since forgiven me for my own mainlanderness. We have too much in common: our propensity for professional self-marginalization, our teaching interest in actual literary creation be it ever so humble, and—unspoken, but overriding everything—our allegiance to the old-time religion of humanist values.

So why am I reluctant to ride along with her on this one?

"Lister's research," she snorts.

"Well that's not really relevant to the proposal, is it? The student—"

"It's all part of the same thing, Hugh."

Lister is interested in postscripts. He believes postscripts are best studied separate and apart from the letters to which they are appended. He is reputed to have developed complex theories about the aesthetics of postscripts and their cultural importance. The humble postscript, hitherto disregarded by conventional scholarship, can say much about a civilization at its most inadvertently self-revelatory, he thinks.

Bernadette is staring at me, daring me to contradict her.

"Uh, times change, right? It *is* 2006. And yes, I am ashamed to say that's all I've got. Sorry."

She's starting to get angry now, though she's struggling to project an expression of goodwill. Haven't we been on the same side for nearly two decades, she seems to be asking. And haven't I long since forgiven her for the satirical poem about a Creative Writing instructor from the mainland named Hubert, who sought to convince his students that publishing outside Newfoundland might be a good thing, and as punishment was tortured and then dismembered by several female spirits of place with unpronounceable names from Irish mythology? Well, haven't I?

What she says is: "I would have expected more of you."

"Look, Bernadette, I don't mean to be flippant here, but the thing is, if we try to draw a line in the sand on this one, we're going to end up looking like twin Canutes with the tidal wave of 1929 bearing down on us. What's the point?"

I'm quite proud of myself for this, the "twin Canutes" idea stressing our putative common cause, and the tidal wave reminding her of my hard-won immigrant's knowledge of all things Newfoundland. But she's not mollified.

"Fifteen years ago, or even ten," she says, "you wouldn't be talking like this. You wouldn't have given up." There's a note of sad reproach here. I'm being reclassified under the rubric of "lost cause." She's ready to make a more serious move toward Beothuk Physio.

"I've seen the future," I tell her. "It has an endless supply of cool T-shirts and an insatiable desire to inflate the importance of the trivial."

But she's already limping away as I finish.

"I agree about the hyphens," she says, over her shoulder.

Driving home along Elizabeth Avenue, I feel a certain low-key guilt-related pang of sorrow at having let Bernadette down. She's right, after all—our profession, it sometimes seems, has been sliding downhill for about forty years now, with increasing velocity lately. But I'm right, too. With three years to go in my career, why bother circling the wagons? No cavalry will come riding over the hill. Chief Lister Craddock and his tribe will prevail. The chronicle of the Battle of Destabilizing Indeterminacy will be written in a language unintelligible to me. But I won't be around to read it anyway.

This thought cheers me up somewhat, as I cruise past a building that used to be a high school but is now, if I'm not mistaken, an old folks' home, nice visual metaphor for the transition I'm about to undergo. A new life awaits, and although it'll be much shorter than the old one, it won't involve making a fool of oneself in front of groups of forty or fifty inattentive twenty-year-olds. What it does involve remains, of course, an open question. But it will be new.

And from this perspective, how unnatural does my professional life now seem. Forcing people to read poems, stories, novels, herding them into classrooms and insisting they pretend to listen to me talking about them. How cruel. And what a disservice to the authors, to their works. As if literature existed to fuel an obsolescent machine in an obscure corner of a factory whose products no one can see. Something out of Orwell. The Ministry of Whimsicality. The Department of Pointless Wordmongering.

Three years to go.

Up the hill on Mayor Avenue, past the cemetery on the left, the new tiny overpriced row houses on the right, past the aging nondescript residential blur higher up (yes, yes, each dwelling no doubt containing its precious cargo of unique misery and—long shot—joy, unknowable to the dilettante passerby), then around the corner onto Freshwater, and home.

Maureen, the love of my life, and "partner" of four years (impossible not to say the word as though there were quotation marks around it) comes out of her study to greet me, face serious.

I'm not sure I'm ready to hear whatever it is she's about to tell me. There's a natural severity to it, her face, the features a tad sharper than what would be considered ideal by whoever it is who determines these things. At first glance there's something formidable in the blue gaze, something in the expression that speaks of prudishness, as in "I have more important things to do than descend to that level." But then you notice the lips, full, lush, sensual despite—one thinks, but for only a moment—the probable desire of their owner.

The shoulder-length dark-blondish hair seems designed to have one's fingers immersed in it. (By "one's" I mean, of course, mine.)

I stand there, besotted. I want to hug her but resist the impulse. (That serious face!) Then she speaks.

"Sandra called."

Sandra is my ex. We've been apart for close to twenty years. Just now she should be regally ensconced in Ontario cottage country with her second husband, Keith. Enjoying martinis on the deck overlooking the lake. No, it wouldn't be martinis. What would it be? I'm drawing a blank. Lemonade, probably, it's an hour and a half earlier there. She doesn't call often.

"They're all right," Maureen says, responding to something in my expression. I know she's referring to my daughter, Emily, and her two kids, as well as Sandra and (last and least) Keith. "But somebody died. I wrote it down." She produces a slip of paper. "Clifford...Clifford MacIntyre?"

Now here's a surprise. Haven't been in touch with Cliff since before Sandra and I split up. I feel a certain pulse of irritation. He's my age. *Was* my age. Where does he get off, doing something like that? It's not time for people my age to die, certainly not people I know. Knew.

Maureen is watching me, tactful.

"Who was he?"

She's wondering if she should throw her arms around me as I high-dive into grief or maybe hold back to see if it's that important after all.

It's a little hard to explain. I knew him when we were kids, in Ottawa. Then much later in grad school at UBC. After having no contact in the interim. Something uncanny there, someone turning up at two widely separated periods in my life, I've always thought, the sort of coincidence that might be allowed once, but only once, in respectably literary novels.

Maureen is waiting for more. In a certain kind of fiction she would be "raising a quizzical eyebrow." Except there's nothing quizzical about her eyebrows even when they are raised, which they're not. Blunt, assertive eyebrows, that's what she has. She doesn't say anything, but she wants to know what happened to the last twenty years.

"Sandra and Cliff's wife, Arlene, were sort of friends, too, so when we moved here it was Sandra who kept up the connection, and then when we split up, well…"

I don't finish the sentence because I don't know how. Why didn't I call Cliff once in a while? Or write. And then when email came in, why didn't I use that?

"I really have no explanation," I end up saying. "I don't know why I let things slide. So what else did Sandra say?"

"Not much. She gave me Arlene's address. In case you want to get in touch. Didn't know much about how it happened, except it was sudden and in a hospital. He was sick and went in for some kind of tests, and something went wrong, she thinks."

So it wasn't anything as arbitrary as being hit by a bus. It was something to do with an aging body ceasing to function. Fuck.

"Feel like a drink? By the way, my new dentist loves my gums. They make her happy."

Cliff MacIntyre, *mon semblable, mon* close-to-*frère*. Well, not that close. And not all that *semblable*, either, except in our boyhood interests and later our choice of profession.

From the ages of eight to sixteen, when his family moved away, we interacted almost daily as classmates, teammates, guys hanging out. No contact for almost ten years, and then from ages twenty-five to twenty-nine, our time overlaps in a doctoral program at the other end of the country. Is there not an aura of significance attending such coincidences? Perhaps not. And now, thirty-plus years later, someone thinks it's important for me to know about his death. No need to ask for whom. I get it.

The image that comes first is of Cliff at fifteen, wearing a torn football practice jersey, the left shoulder pad protruding. The background is vague, suggestive of overcast, wind, and drizzle. It must be the field behind the school, but no one else is present. He's holding his helmet in his right hand as if gesturing to me, but the movement is frozen as though I'm looking at a portrait. I have no idea what the gesture might mean. He's tall, slim, has black hair and brown eyes. He seems about to speak. The jersey is mostly black, but gray around the shoulders. The helmet is green, and I think of the cheer: *Green and white, green and white / For what we want we always fight.* His expression is serious. He's an intense guy, and what he wants to tell me—in this me-produced internal pop-up version of the truth—is important but also (the eyes seems to imply) may be the sort of thing that might inspire a wry smirk.

Possibly it's: *See, there's no more to it than we thought.* Or: *I knew you'd be doing something like this when you heard.* Or: *Have the sense not to make too much of this.* Or: *Wouldn't you know, I got here first.*

We met in the early fifties in a suburb in the south end of Ottawa, the baby boom in full swing, new unpaved streets plunging into wooded areas, new houses springing up constantly, each one seeming to spawn one to six children overnight. The house my family moved into was the second-last one before civilization dead-ended in what we called the bush. Within months the street was a hundred yards longer, and the smell of construction, of clean new wood, was everywhere. We'd collect soft-drink bottles left by the workmen and turn them in for two cents apiece at the nearest convenience store, a twenty-minute trek away.

Cliff was there before me, as were Rex and Jimmy, the four of us at eight or nine forming a natural community, often augmented by others. We'd play hockey on a pond, that cliché of Canadian childhood, not really a pond but a miniature frozen swamp useless to builders, the puck endlessly disappearing into snowbanks, rocks for goalposts, no raising above the knee allowed. The stuff of which bullshit eulogies are made.

As though anyone would ask me to deliver one. And what to say? He was a person of reticence. A man of self-control. He never, as far as I can recall, lost his temper, or acted in a way that was petty or spiteful or intended to wound. He seemed not to function on that level. Would that be enough?

"I can see I'm not making much sense," I say, when I've told Maureen this much.

She's too tactful to agree. She's a poet, too. This town is full of them. During the time I've known her, her work has gradually morphed from a stolid, outdated feminism to something in the ballpark of the mystically gnomic, a realm where the verbal equivalent of silence is oddly sovereign.

If that makes sense. Or even if it doesn't. I can take no credit for this evolution, as she herself is quite capable of pointing out. And now it's okay to hug, the warmth and softness and solidity of her making everything fresh again, as it always does.

It's entirely characteristic of her that, post-hug, she responds to my comment by going for crystallization.

"So if you had to sum him up," she says, "in a phrase or something, the defining quality of his life, let's say, what would you say? Quick, don't think, just blurt it out."

And without thinking I say: "Awkward incompleteness."

In the evening, eightish, the doorbell. Maureen and I in the living room, reading—or, in my case, pretending to read; scattered inconsequential memories of Cliff keep intruding. The ring is followed by a knock, a loud one. We look at each other. I roll my eyes. We know who it is. Or we're ninety percent certain.

"That would be Andy," one of us says, as though delivering the punchline of a long-shared joke.

Andy Lawson, who's lived next door for the past six months, has never figured out our street's unwritten code of etiquette: spontaneous encounters with neighbours are to be conducted courteously but must be brief and superficial. Yes, if in winter someone gets stuck backing out of a driveway while you're shovelling your own, you stop and help to push. Yes, if on a windy day someone's empty garbage can rolls down the street, you rescue it. If an adolescent girl lives close to a house with younger kids, babysitting may be arranged. But that's it. No neighbourhood parties or barbeques, no having people from across the street over for drinks. No casual socializing.

None of this has registered with Andy Lawson.

Several times a week—or so it seems; we don't keep stats—Andy will come to the door, or, if one of us is outside, call over the back fence, wanting to chat, inviting us over ("Who's up for a beer?") or inviting himself over on some pretext ("Can I pick your brains about composting?"), usually cheerful, and always—as far as we can tell—genuinely interested in how we're doing, to the point of plausibly deniable impertinence: "How's your day been? What are you up to?"

None of your business, Andy. Piss off.

No, of course we don't say that. But often we'd like to, or at least I would. Maureen is more hospitable, in large measure because she wants to find out what makes him tick. So far she's been coming up empty. At first she thought it may have been that, as a mainlander (Andy's from Calgary, has some executive job in the oil industry), he was perhaps trying to play the role of some stereotypically gregarious, over-friendly Newfoundlander. But she no longer thinks that, having established that Andy is basically clueless about anything to do with Newfoundland. He seems to have had no preconceptions about the place at all, nor does he seem interested in learning about it. "He hasn't noticed that he's not still in Calgary" is how she put it after a frustrating (for her) conversation this month. "There's a certain bland geniality to him," she's said, and that phrase has become a staple of our Andy-related banter.

He's younger than we are, early thirties, Maureen estimates. And good-looking in a nondescript way, she'll add. I'm not sure what she means by that. He's tall, maybe an inch or two over six feet, but somehow fragile-looking, thin, very slightly stooped. He's bald, his scalp often seeming preternaturally shiny as he peers down at the world. There's an engaging aura of eagerness about him, his facial expressions somehow communicating the idea that he can't wait to see what will happen next. His blue eyes will narrow slightly, evoking the image of a bird of prey focusing on an unsuspecting field mouse, his long nose contributing something to the effect. He claims to have a girlfriend but we've never seen her. She's in Toronto, he's told us, a grad student, will be joining him soon, the date never specified. In the meantime her absence gives Andy innumerable excuses to badger Maureen with questions about traditionally female household matters, details of furnishing and décor, learning from what he calls her "invaluable advice."

Maybe he's just lonely, we usually conclude, though we both suspect there's more to it than that. "Maybe he's just like that." Whatever that means.

All this goes through our minds—or at least mine—when the doorbell rings and the knock ensues.

"You've got the short straw," Maureen says, meaning that I'm closer to the front door so I have to go.

"Howdy!" he says when I open it. I think he's being ironic, but I'm not sure.

He makes as if to move forward, but I stand my ground. Once he's in, he'll be difficult to dislodge.

"Hi there, Andy," I say, hoping to convey *pro forma* politeness underscored by the heartfelt message that trespassers will be prosecuted. And yet, as I say this, I'm filled by the sense that, despite everything, I actually like the guy. It's as though he needs to be there before I can remember that. All of a sudden I don't want to turn him away, don't want to disappoint him.

"Hugh, I've got a favour to ask." He says this in the tone of someone revealing a distant yet disgraceful indiscretion, the sort of thing to be discussed in low and serious voices.

"Yes, Andy?"

"My sprinkler. It's not working. Is there any possibility...?"

"Of course, of course." What a relief. I can take him directly to the shed, avoid the trauma of having him in the house. Maureen will be pleased.

And we haven't made it to the shed before I've spilled the beans about Cliff's death and the unsettling effect it's had on me.

"That's tough," he says. "I guess it'll take a while to process that."

Yes, he says "process." But his heart's in the right place, I'm pretty sure.

He takes the sprinkler away, and I go back inside.

"Thanks for taking one for the team," Maureen says.

Long after midnight, Maureen asleep, I stumble half-awake into the kitchen, open the fridge door, fumble with the orange-juice container. The light preternaturally bright. The roof of my mouth has never known moisture. This is what I get for not drinking anything before trying to sleep. Of course if I had drunk something I'd now be in the bathroom, thinking once again about the Philip Larkin poem about peeing in the middle of the night. In old age.

I don't think he wrote about groping for orange juice in the wee hours. Maybe I'm striking a blow against the death impulse (if it exists), refusing to capitulate to whatever urge compelled him to write.

Cheers, Philip, I think, raising my small glass. Too bad you can't join me.

I remember a TV series Sandra and I used to watch, back in the eighties. One of the characters died suddenly but came back to one of his friends, climbing out of a grandfather clock and spouting a few pretentiously enigmatic lines before disappearing forever. I refuse to let that happen.

Cliff. If you're lurking in the dishwasher, stay in there, okay? I won't even check.

And what should be said in these circumstances anyway? I'd have to go back about a half-century for an answer to that one. Our grade-eleven Latin teacher was a just-off-the-boat Scot (in those days it might even have *been* a boat) called Mr. MacSweetie, whose name was the clearest case of false advertising we'd ever seen. Bright, acerbic, simmering with a sense that his merit would never be recognized in the secondary schools of Ontario, he was, despite his contempt for us, deeply in love with the likes of Catullus, Horace, and company.

"Consider the sound of the phrase," I remember him remarking as we plodded through a Horatian ode. "*Durum est.* It is hard. Yes. *Durum est.* You can hear big heavy doors banging shut. *Durum est.*"

TWO

"Unfortunate unforeseen alteration in domestic arrangements," Terry Foley is saying.

"She kicked you out?"

"Somewhat overstated, but in essence accurate. There was some uncertainty about my faithfulness. Despite the fact that no contract had been signed. As it were."

My ex-son-in-law drains the last of his Guinness and leans away from the table, an expression of self-righteous calm emanating from his mustachioed face, whose cheeks, I'm noticing, are somewhat rounder than they once were. It's been, what, fifteen years now since he was first my student, then my drinking buddy during a bleak patch in my own life, then my son-in-law. Or is it closer to twenty?

In his mid-thirties now, Foley is heavier than he was in his student days but still manages to radiate a sense of raffish self-regard, his blue eyes (despite everything, one might say), retaining the spark that contributed significantly, I've suspected, to his womanizing charm. His dark brown hair is longer than fashionable nowadays, a sign not so much of negligence as of deliberate disregard of convention. I resist the impulse to tell him to get a haircut, not wishing to cast myself as an old man from the 60s, resentful of them damn hippies. He'd look a lot better, though.

"Foley, you were living in her house, *with* her, whatever that phrase means these days. Don't you think that implies…"

Foley sighs. Who's the student now, he seems to be asking. "No, in point of fact, and this must be a generational thing, it implies nothing at all. And in any event, there was no hard evidence, you see. It was all irrational supposition."

I resist the impulse to point out that any such supposition is likely to be entirely rational. Instead I sip my Smithwicks and wait. He's called this meeting, after all. Which means he wants something, and now he knows I know what it is. He'd prefer I be the one to articulate it. So I won't.

If that sounds childish, I'll plead guilty. Sometimes it seems best to deal with Foley in the simplest possible way, using schoolyard techniques learned in my prehistoric past. Say nothing until your opponent caves.

Inevitably the case in point that pops into my consciousness involves Cliff MacIntyre. Our buddy Rex Nairn gets an A+ for a composition assignment, reluctantly allows Cliff and I to read it, a brief fantasy about sinister underwater humanoid creatures who lure unsuspecting children into ponds, streams, rivers, and do not drown them, but subject them to some sort of subaqueous alchemy that turns them into zombie-like replicas of themselves. After explaining this to his young victim, the villainous whatever-it-was chortles in triumph that, in this way, his species will gradually take over the world.

The next day Cliff shows up with a comic book which, as was the custom, included a one-page piece of fiction on the last page. Not quite word-for-word, but close enough. Cliff presents the comic, folded open at the appropriate place, to Rex. Rex says nothing. Cliff says nothing. Rex, the golden boy, the one in every group with the air of unearned superiority, can't afford to admit anything. Cliff, the one who defines himself by his against-the-grainness, the one in every group not bound by its conventions, has nothing to lose. Neither speaks for a long time. The last bell is about to ring. Miss Nelson will soon be leading us in the Lord's Prayer.

Finally Rex cracks. "Coincidence," he says.

Cliff does not mock or scoff. The stranger who's just drifted into town has shown up the establishment for what it is. But it'll all be forgotten by recess. At least until now.

The Duke at warm midafternoon is almost empty. There are a few tourists outside on the deck, but the interior has a deserted-cathedral feel to it, a single VLT player instead of someone lighting a votive candle. A spiritual vacuum where Foley and I enact ritual gestures of camaraderie barely meaningful to ourselves.

"So," Foley is saying. "What I was hoping."

He doesn't need to finish the sentence.

"No."

He looks hurt. "Listen, let me get you another."

This is a sign of true desperation.

"All right, but no means no."

He smirks. "It never does, old boy. It never does." The phrase "old boy" is delivered with appropriate irony, a nod to an earlier era when, as an undergraduate, he was, remarkably, and to the horror of his friends, heard to use it to address a cab driver.

He never did it again. And has been reminded of it so often that it's become a standing joke. "It never does," he says again.

And in this case, he happens to be right. I'm toying with him. Maureen and I will be going to St. Pierre for a brief holiday in a couple of days, so having Foley as a housesitter would be both prudent and painless, and after that, Maureen is off to Saskatchewan for two weeks, a writers' retreat. The idea of Foley as temporary roommate seems amusing. Why not?

Fifteen years ago, as an undergraduate, Foley exuded promise, but where is it now? He wanted to be a poet, as who doesn't at that age? He had academic ability. He met and seduced my daughter, Emily, his one "conquest" (his word, though never of her), who proved so strong that he was the one colonized, Vancouver grad-student father of two, in endless pursuit of his doctoral grail and of sexual partners other than Emily. Who four years ago left him, touching down briefly here before taking root in Ottawa with the kids, Foley following her here and staying, surviving on the fringes of the city's cultural life, sponging off a procession of women, grasping at subsistence-level journalistic crumbs, teaching a course or two at the university, always scraping by, Emily visiting two weeks every summer with the children who seem increasingly baffled as to his identity, a sense of permanent low-key sadness somehow clinging to him like the smell of cigarette smoke, despite his outward good cheer.

Why then am I so hard on him?

He returns with our pints.

"It would only be for a few days, really," he says now, launching a parody of an ingratiating smile in my direction, knowing I'm in on the joke. "By the beginning of next month I'll be able to line people up to share a house with, the new school year and all that, so you needn't torture yourself at the prospect of not being able to get rid of me. Cheers."

"Can you imagine how difficult it would be for me to clear that with Maureen?"

Foley pauses. "My intelligence sources have informed me that she'll soon be departing our fair shores for something like a fortnight. Very soon."

Of course, plugged into local artsy gossip as he is, Foley would know about her writing retreat.

"Our fair fucking shores, Foley?"

He ignores this. "In the meantime, a matter of a few days only, I'm sure you could persuade her...."

"The ground rules would have to be spelled out. On paper. Signed in blood."

"Done."

One thing about Cliff MacIntyre, he never made fun of my deformed right hand, though perhaps "deformed" is excessively dramatic. The fourth and pinky fingers are fused together, as though the fourth finger laboured to give birth to the pinky and never quite finished. Now, of course, it's a minor distraction, hanging about lethargically at the edges of my consciousness, sliding to the centre only when someone takes a longer-than-necessary second peek. Boyhood was a different story, though I developed the necessary defense mechanisms. But there were times when even my closest buddies couldn't resist taking a shot, and that stung most—the crudity of Jimmy McFadden, for example, the least witty of our little group. And even Rex Nairn would make the occasional arch comment about "people with unusual physical conditions."

But Cliff, never. It was as though he didn't notice such things, or more precisely, once they were brought to his attention, willed himself not to notice them. Somehow my warped hand was simply not germane to an interpretation of the world as he understood it. Similarly I can recall no instance of his being petty or spiteful or deliberately hurtful toward anyone. Not that he was an exemplar of saintly detachment. In fact, he was vigorously, even obsessively competitive. No, it was more the attitude of the artist who draws certain of his raw materials from the world around him and can afford to ignore the rest as dross.

How I envy him that ability. Age has not mellowed me, I fear. I'm more conscious now of deformity—physical, moral, aesthetic, spiritual—than ever. In myself and others, but mostly others, Foley being the most obvious usual suspect. But in Emily, too—what deficiency of taste attracted her to Foley in the first place? In Maureen, plugging away at her impenetrable poems that perhaps fifty people will read carefully, though several times that number will buy the book. In my colleagues at the university, about whom (with honourable exceptions), the less said the better. In my own teaching, with its sadly naked attempt to foster a love of reading and writing in my bemused captive audiences.

And of course in my own academic work, the occasion for this self-indulgent digression. I'm labouring over a review, a novel by a woman I've never heard of, though it's her sixth. It's a book that has no reason to exist, the sort of book that makes you feel that, in certain circumstances, book-burning might not be such a bad idea after all. Why am I writing this review? As a favour to the editor of a journal, an old friend who has done me favours in the past and may do so again in the future, whatever smidgen of it is, in my personal case, left. Cliff would have made short work of it. He would have summarized the plot, commented on how the novel is similar to and different from certain other works, avoided explicit evaluation while detailing aspects of what he would have called its "artistry," a semi-derogatory term for Cliff, who believed that aesthetic issues were essentially trivial. Books made statements, as far as Cliff was concerned. The point of studying Canadian literature was, after reading as much of it as possible, to discern what he called "significant patterns" and to interpret those patterns to reveal the country's "national character." No wonder Cliff never got a tenure-track job, quitting in disgust after years of trying and embarking on a second career at forty, in IT.

A Safe Place, by Ernestine Ericson, tells the story of a woman who leaves her cloddish husband (with whom I sympathize, though I'm clearly not supposed to) to live on a tiny island with a lighthouse keeper (who is meant to be a charming, enigmatic misfit, but who is in fact a manipulative sleazeball right from the start). The woman herself is nothing to write home about—she has no mind, no ambition, does nothing for much of the narrative except keep house, stare at the water, and scold her ten-year-old son, who, as one might expect, is bored silly by the isolation, and whines endlessly about the crappy food and the absence of other kids. It does not occur to the woman that this is not the best life for him. In fact not much of anything occurs to her, though she likes to describe the lighthouse guy, as in: "His eyes drank in every inch of my body, which pulsated with longing for his confident touch."

She snoops around, uncovering tidbits about his murky past, until he turns into an abusive sleazeball, just as the worst storm of the winter is bearing down. Will she (and her son) survive the escalating horror?

There is no subplot. There is no wit, no play of ideas. There is only the meticulously chronicled plethora of banal detail, rendered in workmanlike prose over 374 pages.

Ernestine Ericson, the jacket flap tells me, in addition to being one of New Brunswick's best-loved novelists, is a teacher of creative writing. Like me.

***

Maureen, oddly, has no problem with the idea of Foley as a houseguest. Of course she's seen him only when he's been at his most ingratiating, when Emily has visited with their children. He's icily, polysyllabically formal with Emily—who reciprocates in the frigidity department in spades—but goofily down-to-earth with the kids, who seem puzzled and somewhat remote at first but gradually accept him in some sort of hybrid, not-quite-paternal role, the magician hired for the birthday party who somehow has the authority to insist that you eat your carrots.

Having watched this happen for each of the past four years, Maureen has, she now explains, been moved by the effort he makes to "be a dad" as she puts it, attaching only the faintest tinge of implicit snark to the phrase.

"Besides," she adds, "your daughter is a bit of a pain in the hole."

There is no doubt that my daughter is a bit of a pain in the hole, what with the principled pig-headedness handed down from her mother, who is, truth be told, an even bigger pain in the hole. Nonetheless I love my daughter in part for her pain-in-the-holeness, which I perceive as partly not her fault (genetic inheritance) and partly a gesture of defiance in a world in which principle means little. And come to think of it, isn't there a dash of that quality in Maureen herself?

"I agree," I tell her. "And I love her for it."

"In any case, Foley can housesit while we're away. I'm gone right after we get back. Then you can have him all to yourself."

Back in my study, I set *A Safe Place* safely aside, and turn to my other quasi-academic task of the moment, the drafting of a memo to the Headship Search Committee in support of my friend Bill Duffett, who has been serving as "interim" for the past year. The previous office-holder, Reg Pike, quit unexpectedly at the end of his three-year term, and no one stepped forward. Bill, the most amiably apolitical and administratively unambitious of colleagues, was, as chair of the P&T committee, coerced into taking over. Now he's decided to go for a full term, opposed by Alice Plover, who lost out when Pike was chosen, and was, unfortunately for her, about to leave on a long-planned sabbatical when Pike quit.

"Dim-witted" and "tenacious" are the most accurate descriptors for Alice, but trashing her in this sort of document is bound to be counterproductive. Take the high road, Hughie.

Okay. Here goes.

I'm writing in support of Dr. Bill Duffett's candidacy for the headship of the department. I've known Bill since 1984, when I arrived at this university. [Refrain from commenting on the irony of the date.] Over the years I have been consistently impressed by his integrity, his common sense, his decency, his civility, his wit. He is one of the very few colleagues whose judgment—about people, about issues—is unfailingly trustworthy. [I can say all this with an absolutely straight face. Duffett does embody these qualities, in stark contrast to almost everyone else in the department, including Alice Plover.]

The fact that he was drafted, Cincinnatus-like, to become interim Head at a time when no one else wanted the position speaks volumes. [Cut Cincinnatus—pompous, plus Barney Power is on the committee, and he won't get the allusion.] He has no interest in climbing the greasy pole of the university bureaucracy. He became Acting Head out of, believe it or not, a sincerely felt sense of duty. [As opposed, let's say, to the insane desire for self-promotion of an Alice Plover.]

Any assessment of Bill's performance as Acting Head must be rooted in a realistic appraisal of the nature of our department. [And where shall we find that if not right here?] To put the case succinctly: it's a mess—fragmented, dysfunctional, lacking a sense of common purpose or direction. [What oft was thought but ne'er so well expressed.] Bill did not create these problems. [No, generations of reactionary boneheads did that.] No Acting Head could have solved them.

Consider the demographic facts. Of our thirty regular faculty members, about half are aged sixty or over. [Astonishing but true.] In a department teeming with eccentric and 'difficult' colleagues...

Oh, why bother? There are two or three such colleagues on the damn committee itself. I decide to wrap up with more boilerplate praise of Bill—the department has not actually imploded on his watch. And it would be nice to see virtue, or a reasonable facsimile thereof, be rewarded for once in a very long while.

———

At the barbershop, at Maureen's insistence. A quarterly ritual.

Getting a haircut is one of those mundane experiences that can serve as metaphor for some of the more important ones. For a short time you're isolated from the normal context of your everyday life, and you're alone. No one can get a haircut for you.

The shop exists in a time warp. Here we are, *déjà vu* all over again, the same view of the harbour from Duckworth Street, the same interior from a different era—old-fashioned cash register, no credit cards welcome here, and there's not even—a matter of carefully reasoned policy—a telephone. Walls festooned with newspaper photos and clippings from decades past, venerable Newfoundland music on the radio ("Thank God we're surrounded by water"), the same two barbers, one clearly into his seventies, the other perhaps a few years younger than I am, but getting up there too. Up here, I suppose I mean.

I've learned to choose times when there are no other customers. The younger barber, the owner, whose chair is closer to the window, is always at the ready. I can be in and out in ten minutes.

I've been coming here for perhaps fifteen years, and while I'm not one to engage in animated dialogue with barbers, I have over time gleaned a substantial amount of information about the barbering trade from this man, whose name I think is either Fred or Wilf. He comes from a generations-long family of barbers. He's told me about the hard times of the thirties, stories passed down to him about weary barbers who would stay open for impossibly long hours in the hope that a single customer might show up. He's told me that alcoholism is pervasive among barbers. He's told me that when a barber drops a comb, he always says, "First time that happened today," a bit of barber humour, since how would the customer know (or why would he care). But one's fellow barbers would know, and chuckle, anything to relieve the strain of long, long hours on one's feet.

But, characteristic of St. John's, our relationship, Fred/Wilf's and mine, is more complicated than one would expect. Shortly after I arrived here, a slighter, sharper-featured version of him showed up as a student in my first-year night class, remarkable for his poor writing. He seemed not to know what punctuation marks were, and his essays flowed from beginning to end, innocent of both sentences and paragraphs. (Yes, I do remember this sort of thing.) Did he fail or drop the course halfway through? That I can't recall. No way could he have passed, though. And during the fifteen years of our barbershop interaction, neither of us has ever mentioned this earlier time.

Until today, that is.

"You'll be retiring soon, will you, sir?" he says, pronouncing the vowel in "sir" almost as though it were an "a"—no trace of obsequiousness in his use of the word, professional reflex only.

"Couple of years," I say apprehensively. But I've acknowledged the truth of our shared past. Like it or not, he'll want to vent his bitterness about my long-ago maltreatment of him while he has me at his mercy, enshrouded by his olive green tarpaulin.

"Wanted to mention it before you left, sir," he goes on, not bothering to explain what "it" is. And why does he assume that I'll leave? Perhaps I'm unconsciously giving off pheromone-like signals that I'm pining for the mainland? "Must've cut your hair a hundred times, sir, and we've never, ya know, said anything."

I mumble something noncommittal.

"Just wanted you to know, sir, that I knew that you knew sort of thing."

Yes, I knew. And after such knowledge, what forgiveness?

But it quickly develops that no forgiveness is necessary. He seems not to have remembered anything about the course itself—or at least is determined, for both our sakes, not to bring it up. Instead the whole rich chronicle of his other life comes pouring out. He's been a musician, played in bands in Toronto for fifteen years before coming back to St. John's and into my classroom. It had been a tough call. He was at a point at which he'd have to make a decision to commit himself to a life on the mainland or to come home. No chance to make a living as a musician here, not in those days, though for a time he ran a school for drummers (a school for drummers!) and still owns a small recording studio, but barbering is what puts food on the table. He hopes to retire soon himself. His two younger daughters (of four) will themselves be in university before long. Perhaps they'll take one of my courses. We both chuckle uneasily.

One thing's for sure. They won't be barbers.

I try to imagine his life as a barber, not the social dimension, which he's talked about before, the connections made with the downtown lawyers and businessmen, but the actual physical part of it, the expert knowledge, his intimacy with the bumps and ridges of innumerable skulls, his no-choice-in-the-matter close scrutiny of so many faces, so much that is simply and powerfully ugly, veins, warts, tiny scars that only he and a wife or lover would notice, his watching over the years as customers age, get gray or go bald, then disappear.

Seventeen dollars for the haircut and beard trim. I give him a twenty, wave off the change. "Thank you, sir," he says as I leave. "See you again now."

I step out into the street, basking for a moment in a sense of spurious freedom. And then I see Andy Lawson.

He's across the street, the other side of Duckworth, heading east, wearing a business suit that must be way too hot on a day like this. Where's he going? Where's he coming from? I have no idea where he works, probably someplace with a floor-to-ceiling window with a view of the harbour, as befits someone in the oil industry.

And wouldn't you know it, he just happens to glance in my direction. My instinct is to look away quickly, avoid eye contact. I see enough of Andy at home. But there's something more, something I can't put my finger on, lurking in the background. As this realization blossoms, Andy recognizes me, waves, shouts. I cringe, recover, wave back. He makes as if to cross the street, but there's traffic. I wave again, a gesture intended to convey the notion that I'm pressed for time and have to hurry off, westward. Which I then begin to do. Over my shoulder I see his puzzled but cheerful smile, as if to acknowledge that yes, there is a great gulf between us, but why can't we, next-door neighbours after all, make some effort to bridge it? To what end? Oh, perhaps a moment of good-fellowship, a brief, or maybe not-so-brief conversation, depending on where he was going in that uncomfortable suit, what oil-related appointment awaited him—where? The Sir Humphrey Gilbert Building perhaps, only steps away, he's been sent by his oily bosses to wrestle with some federal civil servant over some incomprehensible minor technical matter.

Andy would probably want to comment on the irony of our meeting here, of all places, though such random encounters are not uncommon in our city. This isn't Calgary, I'd tell him, by way of bringing things to a faux-natural conclusion, giving him the opportunity to say that Ha-ha, yes, he'd noticed this wasn't Calgary. Perhaps he would then remember that he had this appointment he had to get to. If not, I'd try to think of a way to remind him, tactfully.

But I'd rather not have to deal with any of that.

So I scoot, or at least would like to think that my actions approximate a sixty-two-year-old's attempt to "scoot" around the corner, and find myself faced with the task of climbing a block up what is reputed to be the steepest hill in St. John's, because my car is parked on the parallel street to the east and I didn't want to walk east on Duckworth for even the half-block that would involve my walking in the same direction as Andy, albeit on the other side of the street, lest he view it as an invitation to cross the great divide.

What the fuck is the matter with me?

Up the hill, then. And then I remember the thing I couldn't put my finger on, the thing associated with Andy, the—wait for it—the dream. Because I've dreamed about Andy, had one dream about him anyway, and maybe seeing him downtown, outside the context I'm familiar with, has brought it to the surface.

This is particularly annoying because in fiction, I tell my classes, the presence of dreams is a sign of authorial weakness, there being, always, other ways to convey whatever information the dream was meant to convey. For my creative writing students, one of the immutable commandments, right up there with show don't tell and no trick endings is: No. Dreams. Ever.

But here in real life there was this dream about Andy, conveying information apparently not available in other forms, even though I'm not sure what that information is.

We're in an orchard, at dawn. We're having an important conversation, though I can't recall any words. The trees are heavy with fruit, various colours, no recognizable species, but it's on fire, all of it! Every piece of fruit has a tongue of flame, pointing upward, but nothing is burning up, neither the fruit nor the branches from which it hangs.

Andy's smiling, as per usual, but his expression is somehow serious, confrontational. Perhaps he wants to hurt me. Certainly he wants something. He doesn't have a weapon, though, at least not open carry. But he has some kind of power. There's something special going on, ceremonial even. Later we'll pretend this never happened. I feel grateful that the fire isn't spreading; everything is nicely controlled. For some reason I'm carrying a flashlight. When I flick it on, its pale light seems absurd, superfluous, given the fact that the sun is getting brighter by the second. In the distance a cock crows. There's something scary about the whole scene, and yet there's also this: in the dream I like Andy. I want to give him what he wants. Even though I'm afraid.

THREE

"Nobody turns left at Goobies."

This is the line that I think of, inevitably, as I turn left at Goobies.

It's Nathan Grainger's line. The context was banal corridor banter inspired by someone's report of a contest: what would be the worst possible first sentence of a novel?

Examined, it reveals much that I find problematic about Grainger, as I try to explain to Maureen. The obvious: Grainger thinks it's hilarious to point out that Goobies is *a funny name*. It sounds funny. Don't those benighted Newfoundlanders realize how funny it is? If they did, they'd surely change it. That's what Grainger is saying: "How droll that I'm living in a place where there's a community named *Goobies*! Laugh along with me, my fellow mainlanders." And Grainger's audience, characteristically, consists entirely of CFAs, Newfoundlanders being a rare commodity in our little corner of the U.

"But you can't deny that it *does* sound funny," Maureen observes.

"Of *course* it sounds funny. But Grainger meant it to be funny *because* of its Newfoundland-ness. Not because it just sounds funny in general."

Is this true? (Yes, it is.) How do I know it? (Close, if involuntary, observation of Grainger over a period of not quite a quarter-century.)

"How do you know why he wants it to be funny?"

"I just do. His spiritual home is some Dogpatch in Saskatchewan. He won't admit that he actually lives here." In this, of course, he is following a long departmental tradition, fostered mostly by the now-retired cadre of Brits, one of whom, Winthrop Crawley, was said to have chosen a particular office because it allowed him to gaze out the window in the general direction of Sheffield (his doctoral *alma mater*), while another, Alec McGregor, was reported to have, after a forty-year teaching career, not yet unpacked some of the books he had brought with him from the Other Side.

Do I have occasion for such self-righteousness? Probably not.

In fact many people do turn left at Goobies, the intersection of the TCH and Highway 210, which goes down the Burin Peninsula, through Marystown, and on to our penultimate destination, the ferry terminal at Fortune.

Not much traffic today, though. It's overcast, not as warm as I can't help thinking it should be for August, my internal weather-evaluator having been hardwired for Ontario summers. Also the landscape at first is standard-issue Canadian Shield, stretches of undifferentiated nothingness, camouflaged badly by its layer of bush. Just like pretty much everything else east of Manitoba. After a time, slate gray water, dead calm, manifests itself to the left, a slender finger of Placentia Bay, though it could be any of a zillion anonymous lakes I've driven past over the years.

Cliff MacIntyre wrote poems about places like this, though poetry was a sidebar to his main life's work. They were derivative, as those of any poet who is primarily a scholar are bound to be. In his case the influences tended to be Northrop Frye's garrison mentality shtick and the early Atwood. He liked to adopt the persona of an explorer or early settler, usually baffled or lost, gotten the best of by wily aboriginals, inhospitable-to-humanity geographical features, or starvation. He published one slim volume with a respectable literary press, then stopped writing poetry (as far as I know, anyway) at thirty-one.

I imagine an ethereal version of him floating somewhere above the car, quietly smiling at the presumption of someone driving through this landscape. *Where do you think you're going?* I can hear him asking from on high. *Will things be better when you get there?*

The one poem of his that has stuck with me is a haiku:

> Loon's dark cry on lake—
> Cold dawn will come soon enough
> Its hard bright fist raised

I remember he showed it to me on a boiling summer afternoon in Vancouver, *circa* 1971. "'Cold dawn' my ass," I think I said. I was sweating from the two-minute walk from the bus stop to our office (shared with three other grad students and located in the basement of the building that also housed the library for the blind). As usual he took no offence, pointing out mildly that the weather on a given day was not germane to his artistic endeavours.

"Anyway," I went on, "hasn't the world heard enough about the dark cries of loons?" CanLit was not my field back then, but I could see its potential as a second string when it would come time to market myself, after the completion of my ground-breaking (in my own mind) dissertation on the Romantic apocalyptic tradition. And I could also already see that the version of the world of CanLit in the process of being constructed by Cliff and his cohorts was, despite its endless expanses of wilderness, a country of dead ends, a huge plastic bubble, strangely claustrophobic.

Like yours *isn't now*, he would be saying, with the ineffable smugness of the deceased.

Think you're going somewhere important? Think again, old buddy. And back then, he'd said, of the loon's cry, "It's not a cliché, it's an archetype."

Maureen leans toward me.

"Why are you muttering 'Fuck you' under your breath?" she asks, clearly concerned that she may be the target.

Soon we're in different terrain, flat and swampy-looking, rain drizzling now, the sky discoloured, thoughts of Cliff displaced by those of H. P. Lovecraft. Perhaps one of those side roads to the right will lead not, as advertised, to the fishing communities with French names (Bay L'Argent, Grand Le Pierre, Jacques Fontaine) but to unnamed clumps of strangely designed dwellings half-immersed in fetid ooze, their chthonic denizens having concealed themselves for centuries from English, French, and Indigenous alike, surviving in human consciousness only in the form of legends and folktales.

"It's creepy along here, isn't it?" Maureen says. "The sort of place where cellphones won't work and the radio goes dead."

"You don't want to be after stopping along here," I reply, imitating the gloom-laden Irish-Newfoundland voice of my colleague Barney Power. "Not on a rainy Friday in mid-August. No."

"Dat you wouldn't," Maureen chimes in.

The desolation makes us chattier than usual, as though our voices are enough to keep the forces of whatever-is-out-there at bay. (A great subject for a MacIntyre poem—the "forces" would of course finally annihilate the humans.) Maureen talks more, fine by me, since she's the expert on St. Pierre, having been there perhaps half a dozen times, and the expert on Frenchiness in general, being *parfaitement bilingue* and even, during our time together, having been employed for almost a year by a local francophone organization.

Finally Marystown appears, an outpost of bland, welcome normality with its gas bars, convenience stores and Tim Hortons. And hey, it's clearing up. Nothing Lovecraftian here, I'm thinking, as we stop for lunch. And afterward, it's more sunny than not as we cruise along the north shore of the Burin.

I tell Maureen the story of Cliff's haiku.

"Needs work," she says. "That last line—'Its hard bright fist raised'—is kind of weak, don't you think?"

"It could use a stronger word to end with."

"'Cocked,' maybe?"

"Cliff wouldn't have used it. He would've considered the sexual implication distracting. He liked things clear and simple."

"See," Maureen says, gathering momentum, "that cry could be orgasmic, and it's a *hard* bright fist, right, so, combine that with 'cold dawn will *come*,'" and all you've got to do is replace 'cold' with something warmer and juicier."

"That's the difference between you and Cliff."

"Not the only one, I hope."

———

There was something reflexively prudish, even puritanical, about Cliff, despite his professedly liberal views. When we met in Vancouver, after having been out of touch for close to ten years, he and Arlene were already married, something about which he seemed neither pleased nor resentful but rather accepting, as though being a husband were a chronic and mildly unfortunate physical condition, something one learned to cope with over time. Not only am I sure Cliff was never unfaithful to Arlene, I'm sure the thought never crossed his mind. Screwing around was for other people, or people in books (but not many of them in the Canadian novels Cliff was studying). He took no position on the morality of such behaviour; it just wasn't for him.

He evinced an amused, anthropological interest in the early stages of Sandra's and my getting together, allowing himself a metaphorical rueful shaking of the head as he watched biology do its inevitable work. Though he was tactful enough not to proffer such a reading. Once he referred to his own marriage as something in which he was "entangled," a word which for me conjured up the image of two amphibious creatures of indeterminate species but with an unusually large number of rubbery limbs, attempting to bind themselves together in as convoluted a manner as possible. I decided it wouldn't be helpful to share these insights, and the subject never arose between us again, ever.

"Marriage," Maureen says, and the tone—there's a pensive, now-let-us-reason-together quality to it—puts me immediately on guard. (But why? What's the big deal?) The word has achieved a kind of *emeritus* status in the four years we've been together, a kind of honourable retirement that includes the perception that it should not, when used, be taken seriously. The questions "Why should it?" and "Why shouldn't it?" are no doubt equally valid.

I still have the scar from the first time Maureen used it, way back in the nineties, our prelapsarian fling at adultery when she was still connected to stolid old Ken. After one of our early trysts, she opined wistfully that "It's not like we want to run off and get married or anything," a faux-throwaway comment which for me was tantamount to a declaration that that was precisely what she *did* want. I agreed it wasn't like that, perhaps too heartily, and the discussion was over. (I had no interest in exploring the implications of the phrase "run off," either.)

In this, our second and public getting-to-be-permanent go-round, the subject hasn't arisen except of course in our observation of the marriages of others. My colleagues at the university offer a range of examples: the sixty-year-old who detaches himself from his fifty-eight-year-old wife to take up with, not the archetypal and largely mythical gorgeous twenty-eight-year-old doctoral candidate, but rather a fifty-six-year-old widow who seems not to represent a major upgrade in either appearance or personality. Though I'm the last person to question the mysterious ways of the human heart, I do join with those (including Maureen) who wonder: "What was he thinking?" And then, having made that decisive step, the happy couple decides to wed. For what specious, bad-faith purpose? To please an aging parent or two? For obscure financial reasons? To massage the delicate sensibilities of the supposedly secular university community?

It's at this point that I will lose Maureen. She will suggest, in a deliberately low-key way, that perhaps such couples wish to make some public declaration of their permanent commitment to each other. That explains the widow, but what about his *first* permanent commitment?

She knows better than to say, "Well, what happened to yours?" One of the lessons I have drawn from "mine" (as she well knows) is that the notion of permanence itself is suspect, that when one thinks in such terms, one is implicitly disrespecting the day-to-day nature of life and love, one is voting to suck the authenticity out of the here-and-now. If what happens every day turns out to be permanent, fine. But let's not presume. And that's what marriage is: presumption. Think of Ozymandias, she knows I'll say.

So instead, she'll say that it's touching to think it *might* be permanent, that somehow, though one or both have failed before, two fallible individuals will undertake that challenge, will plunk the cornerstone of that monument firmly in place, that the brave moment at which they perform that ritual is part of *their* here-and-now, isn't it? And maybe the very best here-and-now possible?

And I have to acknowledge she may be right.

All this goes through my mind when I hear her say "Marriage."

What I say is: "Marriage?"

"Your analysis of Cliff and—Arlene, was it? You barely mentioned her. But anyway. It seems so...repugnant, if that's the word. The taking for granted. The lack of any sense of, I don't know, *adventure* for want of a better word. The notion that it wouldn't even occur to him to cheat. It's all kind of sad, in a way."

"You'd rather he'd cheated?" This is smartass territory, and I regret it instantly. She, after all, was cheating when we were first together, and I feel that thought hover in air somewhere near the rear-view mirror. Another time, and she'd relish the flippancy, but not today.

"No, that's not what I meant," she says, her voice suddenly flat.

"It's just, I'm not sure what you're getting at."

"Neither am I." And that, for the time being, is that.

We're moving through Grand Bank at this point, the day sunny and breezy now, Fortune Bay to our right looking all sparkly, material for a tourist brochure. We've fallen silent (why is it no one ever *rises* to silence?), so I'm left to contemplate whether what Maureen has just said should be troubling. And, more specifically, I'm wondering: does she want me to be more like Cliff or less like Cliff?

And further: should I care one way or the other?

Shortly after that I start to feel just a little ill, not really in a physical sense, though I do feel a tension rising from my gut and somehow spreading like water from a spilled cup through various passageways up to and including my forehead. It's more as if that feeling is generated by what's happening in my head, namely a sensation akin to lift-off, as though the planet I've inhabited for more than six decades is suddenly receding from me in some uncontrollable way that threatens to be final.

But none of this affects my ability to drive the car.

Maybe, it occurs to me, I'm getting ready to die, not from any immediate cause but just in general beginning to lose interest in the world, to distance myself from the details of life as I've known it. (That tiny blue ball down there—did I use to live on it? How odd.)

But I'm still here, not ready to plunge off the road into the bay, quite capable of paying attention to the traffic (the car in front of us is, ironically, a red Focus) and to Maureen, who gives me directions as we enter the town of Fortune, a pleasant-seeming community whose only easily recognizable feature is that every commercial establishment on its tiny main drag seems to be owned by someone named Lake.

But who cares how or why all this is happening? Not me, that's for sure. And yet I'm also conscious that this *is* a species of illness, this way of thinking, however initially seductive. I'm not supposed to be like this. I'm not supposed to think that the world can be left behind and it doesn't matter (or that it can leave me behind and it doesn't matter). When this sort of thing happens to people in novels, they're in big trouble.

See what it's like, Cliff's imagined voice is saying. *Not so difficult, is it? Not giving up all that much, are you? Detachment. The opposite of being entangled. Coming unglued from what you've been stuck to. Your story and you've been sticking to it. But who do you think wants to hear it?*

"We can park here and go in to get the tickets," Maureen is saying. "That building on the left."

And I'm back in the here-and-now, anxious to demonstrate my competence in parking to the woman with whom I may be spending the rest of my life. Or, possibly, may not.

She hasn't noticed anything, as far as I can tell. But who knows. Maureen may have decided it's best not to mention my recent bout of weirdness, figuring that I'm likely to invoke my right to remain silent. Or she may have been in some weird place of her own, a fact she may not wish to explain. Two solitudes yadda yadda yadda—something about protecting each other. I can never remember the exact Rilke quotation (not "quote," yes, I am a pedant), only that in the quasi-literate world of journalism it's always used in articles about Quebec and the rest of Canada, and always given an unwarranted negative spin. Thank you, Hugh MacLennan, you whose Christian name I uneasily share.

Perhaps I should resolve to be more forthcoming, to let Maureen in on this new, Cliff-related dimension of my narrative, as a way of reconfirming my allegiance to the present tense and the solidity of the physical universe. But it might get confused with the marital strand of our Cliff-discourse, the one that led us to that conversational cul-de-sac back on the highway.

And of course practicalities intervene. We have to drive across the street and down a small hill to the staging area near the terminal building to unload our luggage. While Maureen guards our two bags, I am to take the car to a parking lot, following an officious little man (he's perhaps five-two, if that) piloting a minivan, with which I and another passenger—a young woman in a blue Neon—will be transported back to the terminal.

This proves to be trouble, or precisely the sort that makes me wish I was back with detached old Cliff. The parking lot is unpaved, rutted, with large puddles in the empty area in the middle. Its perimeter is a high chain-link fence; cars are parked back-on to it, with just enough space between them to allow for the doors to open and the driver to wriggle out. In other words, I'm required to back into a very narrow space, a task for which I'm supremely ill-prepared. At first I try to beat the system by driving straight in to one of the few gaps in the row of vehicles, but the malevolent dwarf is on me in an instant, claiming that I must back in because then it will be easier to drive away when I return, as though backing out of a space into an area where there are no cars would be more difficult than backing into a space with only a hairsbreadth of leeway on either side.

The young woman with the Neon has already deftly disembarked, having done exactly as requested. Her posture conveys a sense of impatience at my antics.

I recognize that it's demeaning to think of anyone as a "malevolent dwarf," and I feel guilty about thinking so negatively about him. He is, after all, only following the instructions of his superiors. He's probably supporting a family of six with this job. It's not his fault that I'm lousy at backing into a narrow space. Still, there's something deeply annoying about taking orders from such a person.

Finally I get in position. I should be able to back straight in. But I can never back straight in. The little man has stationed himself in front of my Corolla and begins making incomprehensible hand signals—the universal guy-language of vehicle manoeuvering that I've somehow failed to learn. Then he starts shouting: "Cut 'er left, sir" and the like. "Oh no sir, yer too close to that one on the right."

At last it's done. I note that I'm not as close to the fence as the others. "Perfect, sir, perfect," he says, lying through his teeth.

The young woman and I climb into his van, she in front. It turns out they know each other. The last few months have been hard for him because of his mother's death, he doesn't mind admitting. She sympathizes. I of course am pointedly excluded from the conversation, both as an intruder who knows no one named Lake, and, worse, someone who doesn't know how to park his car.

The short man must be at least fifty. At that age, should the death of one's mother be such a blow? Or am I merely demonstrating my hardness of heart, my inability to be a normally functioning member of the human race? And why is the young woman off to St. Pierre on her own? Or is her boyfriend waiting at the terminal, and if so, what does that say about him, he who fails even to attempt to park? She's about twenty-five, I'd guess, marginally attractive in a way that you can bet will somehow fade brutally within a decade, pale skin, mousy long hair, with pert breasts that will see her through the short term—but wait until that mouth becomes pinched in a perpetual frown, wait until the skin becomes coarsened and the waistline expands, then we'll see how you do, my pretty. Mwahahaha.

Thoughts such as these sustain me until we arrive back at the terminal. Maureen, guardian of the bags, seems not to have moved.

FOUR

The ferry is half-full or less. It moves fast. There's not much to see—the featureless coastline of the Burin on the left, nothing at all on the right—a comforting shiny blankness insinuating spurious promises of fresh starts. Inside there's a general impression of cleanliness and efficiency, unlike anything found in its Marine Atlantic counterparts. This is a French operation all the way.

Maureen and I retire to our separate books, the only other diversion being a TV mounted high on a wall facing us, delivering what appears to be a detective show in inaudible French. Of course we could have a conversation, but we seem to have decided: Why bother?

Maureen's book, which I peek at from time to time, is one of those thin, handsomely produced paperback volumes of poetry of the sort that people who attend poetry readings with tiny audiences are guilted into buying. This one is by some young hotshot from Toronto who read at the university a few months back. Maureen notices me glancing over and passes the book to me. I start reading from the top of the page, presumably in mid-poem:

If Strom Thurmond is chaperone
rain can't even be the question.
I'd like to say synapses but it's more like
  hydrophobia.
Well, who knows. As long as Maxwell's whatever—
cat, was it—prefers not to, we're all pretty much
synchronized swimmers on the Greyhound to
  Saskatoon.
I mean, aren't we? Am I right?

I pass the book back and smile. She smiles back. Our smiles mean: we both know this is bullshit, but it's regarded as cutting edge, and anyone who wants to establish herself as a poet in this country had better have at least a nodding acquaintance with it. Besides, the poet's a nice guy; he was fun to have a beer with.

I turn back to my own reading material, a not-quite-random choice from the fifty or so unread second-hand books lying around my study, its main selling point the fact that it's small enough to fit into my jacket pocket: an old-fashioned Penguin Modern Classic, originally priced at 3/6—Cyril Connolly's *Enemies of Promise*. Where did I pick it up and why? Photo of Cyril on the front; he looks jowly and serious. One of the many once-important writers I've never quite got around to when everyone else was reading them, in this case several decades ago.

Maureen makes a face when she sees the cover. "Isn't he the one in the Monty Python song, you know, 'Eric the Half-a-Bee,' something like 'semi-carnally, Cyril Connolly?'"

"Yes, he's the guy." What an unfortunate fate for an eminent man of letters. Was this a gesture of revenge on the part of the Python crew, who were perhaps forced to read Connolly as undergraduates?

"Ho-ho-ho, hee-hee-hee," Maureen says, deadpan.

Connolly proves to be an engaging browse. On Aldous Huxley: "he is most typical of a generation, typical in his promise, his erudition, his cynicism, and in his peculiar brand of prolific sterility." Why do no Canadian critics say things like that? "I quote these as examples of Huxley's writing, of the muse's revenge, but they also show the influence of Proust in all its flatulence." The word "Proust" does sound like a fart, sort of. But along with the one-liners Connolly conveys his passion for good writing, his sense of its importance. He refuses to jump on bandwagons. He gives credit where it's due. I speculate about what he might say about Maureen's poet, but soon give it up to stare out at the blankness for a few moments before returning to the book.

In about an hour we're stepping off the ferry onto the soil, or at least the pavement, of France. We schlep our bags into the customs area, at one end of the government building facing us, where fresh humiliation awaits me. I have neither passport nor birth certificate, only a driver's licence, a fact which incenses the female official, who seems to be auditioning for the role of Kafka's gatekeeper. Maureen intervenes suavely in French, but the uniformed woman is not easily mollified, and insists on speaking English, as though to demonstrate… what, exactly, I'm not sure, but certainly something about the superiority of France and its customs service.

"This doesn't prove he's Canadian," she says, waving my licence at Maureen. She seems in the mood for this girl-on-girl conflict. She's small but feisty-looking with a clichéd French face, nose in the de Gaulle tradition. I might as well be a piece of luggage at this point. We have been assured, I think Maureen responds (since she's speaking French now, I'm guessing at some of this), by the people in Fortune, the very people from whom we've purchased the tickets, that a driver's licence is all that is necessary (though Maureen herself just happens to have brought her passport along).

"We decide who gets in," the woman says firmly. She pauses, but then, having made the professional judgment that I pose no threat to the security of *la Republique*, she declares herself the winner and waves me through with a gesture that would be a slap if a face got in the way, a signal of begrudging, graceless magnanimity.

Emerging from customs, we find ourselves in what looks like the official centre of town, with a parklike strip of lawn, trees, benches, a couple of cannons, and a carousel separating the government building from everything else. The whole place looks like a movie set, maybe even a movie set representing a movie set, as in a French knockoff of *The Truman Show*. Or a European version of *The Prisoner*, the old TV series with Patrick McGoohan, a British secret agent spirited away to a mysterious "village," where he is subjected to non-violent but insidious social conditioning for something like twenty-six episodes, maintaining his heroic individuality throughout, never allowing himself to be seduced into giving his allegiance to its artificially organized society—the whole thing a parable, according to righty ideologues, of the failure of socialism to corrupt the human spirit. (The authentic human spirit, that is, Western and capitalist.) Maureen and I stop for a moment to orient ourselves.

There's no doubt. Something about the place declares: This is not real.

But it probably is. Maureen asks directions of a passer-by, who seems not to be an actor, and we discover that our *pension* is only a couple of short European-villlage-y blocks away, and we're there in five minutes.

Later the sense of unreality returns. We spend the last chunk of the afternoon wandering around the town—narrow streets, punctuated by small shops, all of which Maureen insists on exploring. In the stationer's window a poster seeking information about a missing woman, whose face bespeaks a profound sadness, so strong as to suggest she may have had some foreknowledge that something bad was on the way. How can someone just vanish in a place this tiny? "The sea," Maureen suggests. "Over a cliff."

But then why bother with posters? Someone must think there are other possibilities. And there's something in the woman's face that speaks of dignity, as though the source of her sadness is something unalterable that has stripped away her ordinariness, but she has steeled herself to confront it and this has conferred on her an aura of bittersweet beauty.

Beauty, a word I don't often use, come to think of it.

We pass a furniture store, chairs and tables outside on the narrow sidewalk, the prices in euros. No customers.

And what sort of market would there be? A population of 6,000, no economic base, no reason for anyone to move here from France (though of course, technically this *is* France). "Probably all subsidized," Maureen says.

"And why are there so many cars? There's no place to go." Neither of us has an answer for that one.

Ten minutes from downtown we find a large supermarket, half the items on the shelves straight from France and the rest from Canada, Sobeys house brands predominating. We buy cheese, bread, and wine to take back to our room. Just outside we encounter a tall obese young man, perhaps eighteen, dressed in a gray track suit, staring at the ground, locked in sad eccentricity. On the way back, taking side streets so as not to retrace our steps, we run across people gearing up for a wedding—young men in white suit-coats, several shiny cars of French make with balloons and streamers, older women strutting fussily, giving orders. We pass by as though we were ghosts.

Dinner at a restaurant someone has recommended to Maureen. Low ceiling, posters of France on the walls. Only one other table is occupied, people in their twenties, everyone smoking, a colourfully attired toddler in a highchair. A general air of relaxed affluence. The food is excellent. We try several exotically named mixed drinks and head for bed, too old to be checking out the nightlife.

What have we talked about? The strangeness of the place, the strangeness of other people, our own strangeness, none of it with any depth of seriousness. "Four years," we say, shaking our heads as if we're acknowledging our commingled strengths, our stick-to-it-iveness, as though it were an entity separate from us, veterans of a war we had no voice in starting, and the outcome of which remains unclear—but we're alive! Alive.

We've devoted some attention to the missing woman on the poster. Maureen, too, thinks she's beautiful. It seems she reminds both of us of someone, but we can't figure out who. And of course it's possible we're thinking of two different women. Her image is the last thing I remember before sleep.

Morning and we're served breakfast by a middle-aged woman with a limp, who, it develops when Maureen engages her in conversation, has serious health problems that require her to fly to St. John's for treatment every couple of months, everything paid for by the French government, she explains. We're almost alone in the small dining area, a couple from France (Maureen can tell from the accent), fiftyish, the only other patrons, she looking unnecessarily stylish in ways I can't hope to describe. Why they've come here is a mystery, perhaps, we speculate, to fulfil a misguided desire to see every last obscure fragment of their country.

We munch our croissants and make plans. It's sunny and warm. Everything has been simplified. Our day will be spent together, as few of our days actually are. Our goal is to stave off boredom until bedtime, roughly fifteen hours away. We're a team.

It occurs to me that perhaps this is what Maureen had in mind in promoting this expedition. A melting away of the St. John's routine of cohabitation, with its cargo of people and activities that have the common denominator of distracting us from our coupledom. Let's see how we survive without those props. Castaways. Strangers in a strange land. To mention this would be counterproductive. Maureen hates straightforward, let's-see-what-we've-got-here discussion as much as I do. But maybe this weekend is a test. Or, more likely, this train of thought is all nonsense. Witness this morning's relaxed and tender lovemaking. Better to do the *carpe diem* thing and assume the big picture will take care of itself.

We're among the first to climb on the tour bus that leaves from the central square, right near the merry-go-round, every couple of hours. Here we are, tourists doing a quintessentially touristy thing on a day of perfect touristy weather. Maureen, by the window, leans into me for a moment, allowing me to get a good sniff of her slightly-too-dark-to-be-blonde hair. The lovely smell of shampoo in the morning. The deception of the fresh start. And now she's produced a notebook from somewhere, straightens up and starts jotting. I know better than to ask. Or peek. Poem-related, I'll bet.

The driver (another small man, perhaps cognate to the parking guy in Fortune, but much older) announces that his commentary will be in both French and English. The bus gradually fills up with francophones, who, Maureen informs me in an undertone, are, by their accent, all Quebecois.

We head off along the waterfront (impeccable grass, ornamental-looking cannons pointed in the general direction of Burin). "We used to shoot cannonballs at Newfoundland, but now we shoot croissants," the guide announces, setting the tone: how past glories have been tragicomically undercut by forces beyond the control of anyone living here.

We take a left and pass by, if I'm not mishearing, the only gas station on the island. "Six thousand people, four thousand cars," the guide says.

"But there's no place to go," I say quietly as this information is delivered in French.

"Unfortunately, there's no place to go," the guide is saying calmly. "Twenty kilometers of road on the whole island." The tone suggests that he, too, is as bemused by this quirk of his fellow citizens as he expects we will be. Again I think of *The Truman Show*, Jim Carrey watching the same two or three cars incessantly circling the block.

We pass the apartment building that houses the *gendarmes* and their families, regular French police stationed here for two-year tours of duty. "I bet they're thrilled to pull this assignment," Maureen murmurs. "Imagine coming here when you've lived all your life in France."

As the bus moves on, it becomes evident that the most interesting aspect of this experience is going to be the guide's commentary. His approach is the obverse of boosterism. Instead he seems to delight in focusing on St. Pierre's complete failure to have found a reason to exist in this, the post-fishery era.

There's no significant economic activity other than that underwritten by the French government. Nearly all citizens with full-time jobs are civil servants, and nearly everyone else depends on direct government support. Local contractors do very well on make-work projects which stimulate employment. There's plenty of new construction, though the population isn't growing despite incentives for young couples to have children, and for those who've been educated in France (at government expense) to return. Apart from the fishery, long defunct now, there has never been a reason for people to live here. (That warehouse was used by Al Capone's gang during Prohibition. Times were good then.)

No food is grown here. That which doesn't come from France is shipped in from Halifax every couple of weeks. Otherwise people would starve. There used to be some farming, a century or so back, but not anymore. The island is basically volcanic rock, anyway. There's no soil to speak of. You can see how barren the land is now that we're outside town. Yes, there are scrubby bushes, and yes, people have planted trees as a windbreak around their houses, but that's about it. Water collects in pools on that bare-looking hill and drains down to the reservoir on the right, the community's water supply.

We stop at a place where we can see the island of Miquelon across a narrow channel. It's much larger than St. Pierre, the guide says, but only a few hundred people live there, again for no reason related to economics. Perhaps the bright lights of St. Pierre are too much for them. Also, we're told, residents of St. Pierre have summer places over there, as though to demonstrate their determination to parody every last aspect of middle-class Western society.

We shuffle around with our fellow passengers, all of us assuming, I suspect, that when a tourist bus stops, there must be something deemed worth seeing. Except there isn't. The joke is on us. Is our guide perhaps a Zen master in disguise? He's already told us that ninety-five percent of those who live here are Catholics, but that leaves about three hundred in the category of "other." Perhaps there's a secret Buddhist community, dedicated to leading tourists to achieve *satori* unexpectedly?

But after fifteen minutes or so we wander back to our seats unchanged. We pass the guide's ancestral homestead, where vegetables once were grown and animals raised for slaughter, for the butcher shop in town, but "not anymore," this phrase pronounced with a fatalistic wistfulness. No one asks why. Can the soil have deteriorated so much in less than a century, or does it have to do with the will of the inhabitants?

We stop at a lookout on the northwest side of the island, where stunted trees lean inland, crippled by the wind off the Gulf of St. Lawrence. I, alone, of the people shuffling around, am attacked by a swarm of tiny flies, perhaps because I'm the only one wearing a bright orange shirt. "Les mouches," exclaims the woman next to me. Maureen hustles over to do some swatting.

"*Les mouches*, wasn't that the title of a Sartre play, reworking of a Greek tragedy or something?" Maureen doesn't know, but I'm pretty sure I read it (in English translation, of course) as an undergraduate in Ottawa.

It comes back to me as we climb down the steps to the bus. Woodrow Gordon's Modern Drama course, Ibsen to Pinter, *The Flies* coming towards the end, just before Genet. Gordon was a strange guy, we thought, a "confirmed bachelor," often seen drinking alone in such downscale bars as the Albion. But he avoided scandal. There were no sightings of young male friends, nothing at all. Which, for all I know, may have been the bottom-line truth, and if so, how sad.

"Cheer up," Maureen says, as we wait in line.

We pass by the airport, a new one, the guide says, fit for transatlantic flights, though of course there are none. From St. Pierre you can fly to St. John's or to Montreal. At the moment there appears to be not a single human being at the terminal. The runways of the old airport have been torn up, and, where they used to be, new houses are being built, more work for local contractors. From here—we're on a ridge—we can see the shape of the bay and the low hills that shelter the town from the wind. It may not look like much, he says, but France gave away something like half of North America in a treaty with England, in order to retain jurisdiction over St. Pierre and Miquelon. It was all about fish.

Our last stop is the cemetery. It's European-style, everything above ground, row upon row of whited sepulchres. We disembark. Hi there, Mr. Death. Or M. Le Mort, I should say. Nice to see you here in Samarra. Your name is legion, though here all the varieties happen to be French. All those different dates, too. You're pretty much everywhere, aren't you? And every-when. Where is thy sting, the apostle asked. Where is thy victory? Right here, I can hear you saying. *Si monumentum requiris, circumspice.*

Our fellow tourists seem to be more sophisticated consumers of death. They move slowly, inspecting inscriptions, commenting on who knows what details, as though contemplating a major purchase at Canadian Tire. Perhaps they're looking for distant familial connections. Maureen, too, seems to be into it, at some distance from me. Scrutinizing a particular inscription for what seems to me a long time. Writing something in the notebook, hair moving gently in the breeze. Something almost intrusive about it, as though she's violating the privacy of the deceased, scrying the poem hidden in the stone, the letters, the dates. I feel an impulse to go over and touch her arm or shoulder, as though to make sure she doesn't get lost, doesn't wander too far away from the world of sunshine and flesh. But maybe this is how you're supposed to act as a cemetery-going tourist. Be cool. It's only death. It's a ten-minute stop on a bus tour around an island notable only for its obscurity. A bush league Patmos, yielding no revelations today.

The bus deposits us next to the merry-go-round in the town square, patronized by a few squealing kids and their bored mothers. Young men lean against their shiny cars. Hardly anyone walking by. A general air of indolence.

"What now?" I say to Maureen.

"Good question."

After some discussion, we decide to eat.

It's later and we're drinking wine, perhaps too much wine, in what I suppose is a bistro. It's dark and almost empty, and there's a residue of last night's smoke in the air. The barman is fat and balding, his face impassive but somehow communicating a sense that he would prefer we were not here, no, more than that, he would prefer that we did not exist.

But he remains at his station and supplies alcohol on demand, all we require. I'm focusing for the moment entirely on Maureen, the physicality of her presence, the physicality of our coupledness. How much of what we are depends on the sharing of skin, on the coalescing of what has been separate, the generosity of union, the flamboyant spill of self, the austere and delicate taste of otherness. Yes, definitely too much wine. Our respective skeletons buried in flesh, biding their time, waiting for the long warm-up act to be over. But doomed never to know each other. Hard to believe, as we sit at this moment.

I touch Maureen's forearm, lightly. She smiles, raises the glass to her lips, swallows. I think of the wine plunging down her throat, I stare at her throat as I do that, she follows my gaze down to her shirt, she smiles again, assuming I'm staring at her breasts, which I am, of course, thinking of how much I've cherished them, how often I've used them to give her pleasure, how they've given me pleasure, how powerfully they bring us together. I also recognize how drunk I've become.

It's *non sequitur* time. The conversation is allowed to meander where it will, but the subtext is that our bodies are connected, have been, will be again. We replay some of our greatest hits, but our history keeps congealing into the present, our legs making contact under the table. How providential that we're both wearing shorts. Leg against leg, hand (mine) on thigh (hers).

Thighs, thighs. Where are the love poems that praise female thighs, surely one of God's greatest, if unsung, gifts to humanity? Maureen's thighs now, for example, warm, exquisitely shaped (I'm biased, probably, but they all are, every female thigh I've seen, pretty much), icons of sensual perfection. (You're talking nonsense, Hughie. I know. I'm drunk, okay? I'm allowed.)

Then someone from across the room shouts "Hi folks! Fancy meeting you here."

"Oh for Christ's sake," Maureen mutters before Andy (for of course it is he) can make his way to our table.

For an instant I get the sense that he's been "viewing" us, Maureen and me, as though we were an installation in a gallery. He's wearing a short-sleeved shirt of a urinous yellow that calls attention to itself in a mildly annoying way. He looks somehow puzzled but respectful, and hesitates for a moment, as though weighing the possibility that we're not going to be as welcoming as next-door neighbours should be. But then he decides that such speculation is absurd and moves briskly toward us.

"Certainly a coincidence, a happy one I hope," he says with unnecessary heartiness. Then he decides to extend his hand toward me. "Dr. Norman, I presume. And of course Ms. Finnerty." He sits down, still shaking my hand (and yes, when we let go, he discreetly checks out the deformity, though he's seen it before, of course; we've never mentioned it). "Mind if I join you?"

"Do we have a choice?" I hope that jocularity will override annoyance in the tone.

"Not really." He seems somewhat too happy to have found us. "My, you two look cozy. And you're almost out of wine. Why don't I get you some more?"

"Actually, Andy, we were thinking of calling it a night."

But then Maureen chimes in. "But I think we can hang in for a while, can't we? Why don't we switch to beer. One last round."

Andy grins at her, springs to his feet and heads off to the bar. I look Maureen in the eye. "What?"

"Well, it's kind of sad he came here all by himself. Who does that? We can put up with him for a few minutes, can't we?"

"You're right in love with him, aren't you?"

She kicks me as Andy returns with three Stellas. He's noted the kick but doesn't say anything.

"Hope Stella is okay. I guess I should have asked. But since we're in France, I thought a French beer."

"Actually, it's Belgian," Maureen says, somewhat prissily. She enjoys scoring points in this way.

Andy looks at each of us in turn. He's almost completely bald, and his head seems unusually shiny this evening. Or maybe it's just that I've had too much to drink.

"Belgian," he says, as though considering whether to believe it or not. "Well, that's interesting." He's quiet for a moment, as if pondering the importance of this fact. Then, out of the blue: "Hey, did you guys see the poster of that missing woman? They're all over town, I've seen five or six just walking around."

"Yes, we did. We noticed how sad she looked, as if she knew what was coming. If in fact it was."

"Haunted, almost," Maureen puts in.

"That's what I was thinking," Andy says. "How sad. My heart goes out. This is a sad little place, really, isn't it? On the basis of having been here since this afternoon." For a moment he seems genuinely sad. But then he says, "Of course she could still be alive. Stranger things have happened." And now he seems genuinely to have perked up. I feel, bizarrely, happy for him. And I remember how natural it seemed for me to tell him about Cliff.

"So, Andy, what are you up to? Coming here, I mean?"

He waits for a moment, as if he hadn't really thought about it before. "Well, I like having new experiences. I thought this place would be interesting. I mean, you know, a tiny outpost of France in the middle of nowhere. What's that all about? The French government basically bribing people to live here and vegetate. To be blunt. And you know what it reminds me of?" He stops here. Apparently we're really supposed to figure out what it reminds him of.

"No, Andy, what?"

"Newfoundland." He pauses, his expression somehow innocent in its confidence that we'll have to give him credit, that he's really nailed it.

Instead no one says anything.

"Not," he adds hastily, "that I mean to be insulting to Newfoundlanders, especially not you, Maureen. But really, there's the oil industry and nothing else, right? In terms of the economy, I mean. Nothing else major, anyway. And here, there's nothing at all. But there will be." He leans forward, as though to prepare us for an important personal revelation. "The Laurentian Basin," he says. "Due south of here. Eight or nine trillion cubic feet of natural gas, seven hundred million barrels of oil. And the French own a corridor that cuts right through it. No drilling yet, but when it happens, they'll be there. It's all about the oil. And the gas. Just like Newfoundland."

"So," Maureen says, "their share of the oil and gas justifies pouring millions into this place forever?"

"Pretty much. What makes the world go around. In one sense." He smiles, as if considering whether to tell us in what other senses it goes around, and what makes it happen. But then thinks better of it.

Back in our room as we get ready for bed, Maureen tells me that she thinks the oil and gas thing is a red herring. "I'm sure the stuff is there, but who knows if it'll ever be feasible to get at it. And what percentage of it belongs to them anyway?" She thinks the real reason the French continue to support St. Pierre is that they would lose face if they backed away. "I mean, they're pretending it's part of France, right? Think of the humiliation if they gave it up. And who would they give it up to? You heard the tour guy. They can't do a thing on their own here. Can't even feed themselves. Even if they do know how to cook."

"Maybe there's be a referendum and they'd join New-foundland," I suggest. I'm already in bed. Maureen has just emerged from the bathroom.

"And we would want them why?"

"We couldn't stand to see them starve, right? Newfound-land hospitality, sure."

I wait for a response, but Maureen has lost interest in this topic. "It's not that late, is it? You're not really tired, are you?"

FIVE

"That phrase you used to describe your dead friend—'awkward incompleteness,'" Maureen is saying.

We're on the ferry back to Fortune, drinking coffee from Styrofoam cups. Moving back toward the real world, I'm guessing, given the drift of the conversation.

"What about it?"

"I keep thinking it could apply to me."

"Why do you think that?" This is a surprise. The phrase about Cliff just popped into my head when she asked me about him. I've almost forgotten I said it. I have no idea why she would think it has anything to do with her.

"Look at my life," she says. "What have I done with it, really? You know? I've brought up one child, I've been through one bad marriage, I've had a bunch of different no-name jobs, I've written two slim volumes that no one will ever read. Not much to show for almost half a century. So incomplete for sure. But also awkward, as in no coherence, no grace, no elegance. Just stumbling around."

"Well, mine isn't any more impressive, when you look at it that way. Probably everyone is awkwardly incomplete, from a certain perspective. But why look at it that way? Why keep score? Why lust after style points? Who says your life should be structured like an epic? Maybe it's a series of brilliant fragments. Maybe intensity is what you should focus on."

"Maybe," she says. She wants to drop the subject. No pep talks, please.

But I'm already well on the way to believing my own bullshit.

"No, really. And as for that awkward incompleteness thing about Cliff, that's totally different from you. In a sense he never got to do what he really wanted to, at least in the way that he should have. Trained to be an academic, busted his ass for ten years at academic shit jobs, published more than most full professors, but then gave it up because he couldn't get a tenure-track job."

"Why was that?"

"That's where the awkwardness comes in. He wasn't impressive at interviews. He didn't seem like the kind of guy who could socialize well. He was adamant about saying what he believed, telling the truth as he saw it. But more than that, he somehow never could quite fit in with any group he was associated with. Or wanted to, for that matter. So that's not exactly you, is it?"

I have the feeling that I'm being perceived as trying to browbeat her into submission, the last thing on my mind when we started this dialogue.

"Not exactly," she says. "But there are similarities."

I decide to leave it at that. But is there anyone who isn't a naïve egotist who can analyze his or her life in such terms? Opportunities missed, potential unfulfilled for reasons beyond one's control. Of course there are plenty of naïve egotists around, and therefore presumably lots of folks who imagine their lives to be graceful and complete. How lucky I am, I think, that Maureen is not one of them.

And what a strange conversation this has turned out to be. But it seems now to have run its course. Maureen is no longer in the mood. She takes our empty coffee cups to the nearest trashcan, comes back, and, indicating the book on the seat beside me, says, "So, what's Cyril after saying?" The "after" is of course a joke, the educated Newfoundlander self-consciously using the vernacular to distance herself equally from her cultural past and her educated persona: she herself doesn't speak like that except ironically, but she hasn't forgotten how people really talk.

Earlier I'd been flipping through *Enemies of Promise*, checking out a sentence here, paragraph there. "Here's a good one. Connolly was at Eton with George Orwell. He mentions that Orwell, at eighteen, was beaten by the prefects for being late for prayers. Who knew?"

Shortly after this a woman approaches us, focusing on Maureen, making the womanly noises appropriate to greeting someone not encountered for a long time. ("Maureen? It *is* you, right? You haven't changed a bit!")

The woman is about my age, and I'm sure I've met her before. When we make eye contact, she does a double-take, and gushes at me, too. "It's Eleanor. Eleanor Atkinson?"

And then I remember, shortly after moving here, a dinner party at my colleague Barney Power's place. Enough information to make the connection between this woman and her twenty-years'-previous incarnation, when she was about forty and newly split from her philandering chiropractor husband. I remember thinking she looked good in a straightforward no-frills way, that her next partner would be a lucky guy (a thought I chose not to share with Sandra, my then-spouse). Now, predictably, the roundish face has somehow imploded, though the brown eyes are clear and amused-looking. Amused at me, probably, noting a parallel deterioration in my own face.

And I remember almost nothing about that night except that Eleanor had been a patient at the hospital that Barney's physician wife worked at, and she had been mentioned at some staff meeting under the initials "E. A." as an example of "difficult intubation." When Marie Power told this story—it was news to Eleanor at the time—Eleanor accidentally snapped the stem of the wineglass she was holding. Stains, embarrassment, laughter.

So now I respond to her greeting with, "Ah yes, difficult intubation," and she laughs, recognizing that one ridiculous thread connecting us across the decades. I have no idea what intubation is.

Maureen, it turns out, has known Eleanor in a completely different context (co-workers at the Newfoundland tourism 800 number in the late eighties), and that largish, somehow spongy-looking man standing a few feet away with a vaguely proprietorial air is Henri Poirier, one of St. Pierre's leading businessmen and her husband of some five years. ("He's also developing properties in St. John's, in the downtown," Eleanor

71

says.) But Maureen and Henri have met before too, at some social event associated with Maureen's old job with the francophone organization. Everybody knows everybody (except for me and Henri, until now). A typical St. John's moment.

After a few minutes the exaggeratedly friendly woman-talk dries up and the Poirier-Atkinsons disappear. And we discuss the potential whys and wherefores of their union, not ungenerously, we hope.

The drive home is uneventful.

Foley is there to welcome us, grinning mock-obsequiously in the manner of a faithful retainer in a hypothetical British sitcom. "As you can see, the integrity of the dwelling's structure is unimpaired. I'm sure you'll see your way clear to returning the damage deposit." There's an unusual upbeatness to his delivery of this limp repartee, and it flashes on me that he must have successfully launched yet another relationship over the weekend. Probably right here. In my house. On my sheets.

"What you are no doubt surmising is correct. I can read it in your face. I did have a dinner guest yesterday. I trust that will ruffle no feathers." He nods in the direction of Maureen, who, after a friendly hello, has bustled past him in the direction of the nearest bathroom.

"No fear," he says, *sotto voce*. "I've laundered the sheets. As you instructed. The one task I have not completed, however, and I urge you to permit me to do so now, is the washing up. The meal I prepared—inspired by traditional Syrian cuisine—required the use of a number of pots and pans, not all of which have as yet been scraped into pristine condition."

"Feel free."

There's a pause. "And," he continues, "I assume our agreement…is still in effect?"

"Agreement?" I almost hate myself for doing this, but not quite.

"That I might…prevail upon your hospitality.…" In another era, he might be tugging his forelock. I recall Sandra's acerbic judgment, delivered immediately after their first encounter: "Oh, I can see that he'll bow and scrape, all right." This memory causes me to smile, and to realize that this has gone on long enough.

"Yes, yes. Of course."

"Ah, excellent. I had feared, you see…"

"Till the end of the month only. You get the middle bedroom. The small one. With the single bed."

"Got it, got it. In any event, I expect not to be burdening you with my presence, except intermittently, assuming things continue to go well. This evening, for example, a tryst has been arranged. Not for here."

"Good luck."

Email. Delete the spam and there are five real messages. Two from students inquiring about the syllabi for my fall courses. There's nothing on the departmental web page, they politely observe. Could I enlighten them? Not just at the moment, I'm afraid.

One from another student, fifteenth on a waitlist, wondering if I couldn't see my way clear to letting her jump the queue, given that she's a single parent with diabetes who really needs this course to get into Education. No. Experience teaches that such a student, if taken in, will prove to be more miserably incompetent than the weary norm. There are limits to charity.

Two *actual* real messages, then. One is from Arlene MacIntyre. I don't feel up to reading that one just yet. I can't believe it will be accusatory, but where have I been for the last twenty-plus years? And now it's too late. No, I don't want to deal with those unspoken questions today, thank you.

The last message is from Raissa McCloskey, nationally acclaimed filmmaker and former creative-writing student of mine, contemporary and friend of Emily, and personification of the life-force. "Need to bounce some ideas off you," she writes. Yes, my love. You just bounce away now. As hard as you like. I'll cherish the bruises. Tomorrow at eleven, as you suggest. See you then.

Morning and Maureen is busying herself with preparations for departure. She leaves tomorrow, stays with friends in Toronto for a couple of days, then on to her writers' retreat in Saskatchewan.

Foley, it seems, has spent the night elsewhere.

It's time to steel myself to read Arlene's email. I'm relieved to note there are about twenty addressees, presumably those of us from the remote fringes of Cliff's life who are deemed to merit a detailed account of what happened. I note that Sandra is on the list, though most names I don't recognize. Arlene's narrative style is straightforward, laced with understated frustration and anger. As I read, I think that, in similar circumstances, I could never react so temperately.

...Unfortunately in spite of two trips to the doctor in the week prior to his death his illness was never treated seriously. I tried very hard to advocate for him and push the doctors to take his complaints seriously. Cliff was undergoing testing with a hematologist and we knew he had an auto-immune blood condition that was compromising him. It was not life threatening but it was aggressive enough that his spleen was enlarged and he had what was called hemolytic anemia.

So when he developed a severe sore throat on the Monday I pushed him to go to the doctor. I even went with him and when the doctor suggested that the sore throat was a viral infection I pushed for them to do a throat swab and I also reminded him of Cliff's two ear infections with perforated eardrums in the past ten months which were never taken very seriously.

I did manage to get a throat swab for strep infection ordered which came back negative. However, Cliff just got progressively worse all week and finally I took him back to the doctor on Friday. He just said, "It's a virus. It's just going to have to run its course." He gave us a prescription for an antiseptic mouthwash. This was in spite of the fact that Cliff had complained about how the pain had moved from his throat to his neck, and that he'd developed a cough with severe pain in his chest. When I took him to the hospital the next morning he was in such pain that every breath hurt. He was running a fever, his white blood cell count was up and he had a shadow on his lung in a chest X-ray. He died on Sunday.

The cardiologist at the hospital said that his death will probably remain a mystery that medical science can't explain. But I suspect that the pathology report will show that mistakes were made, serious ones. I intend to pursue this wherever it leads…

My first thought is, So it can happen that fast. As if I'd never heard about any of the much quicker deaths available to everyone. That fast, and nothing can be done, or nothing that can be done *is* done. A world of dim-witted bystanders, except for the odd ineffectual advocate.

And at what point did Cliff know? This is a question that Arlene's account doesn't address. And how did he handle it when he did know? Atheist to the core, he wouldn't have flinched, I'd be willing to bet. No deathbed histrionics, external or internal. Maybe a last joke at his own expense, though he might have been in too much pain to deliver it aloud. But he'd be thinking it. I'm sure he would.

"Okay, here's my idea," Raissa McCloskey is saying. "There's this guy, he's a novelist, I'm thinking of Aaron Spracklin for this role, I think he's finally ready for it, he's trying to write the great Newfoundland novel, right? The character, I mean, not Aaron."

We're having coffee in one of those downtown coffee places. No doubt they're all different, but as soon as I step into one of them, I forget which it is. Physically Raissa, as usual, dominates the room. There's her sunburst of auburn hair, for one thing, slowly darkening as she gets older, now (she's thirty-four) somewhat understated but still head-turning in itself. There's her clothing, which somehow creates the impression of an exploding rainbow, exotic enough that sometimes (she says) servers will ask whether she's a tourist from a cruise ship. And there's her *presence*, something about her that declares that what is happening here is real, is worth paying attention to.

"So Aaron, or at least his character, is trying to write this novel, and he's obsessed by this one image. You know there's this old German folktale, at least I think it's German, I haven't researched it yet. Or maybe it's not a folktale, maybe it's just a saying, sort of like a proverb or something."

I'm thinking: Raissa McCloskey at twenty, showing up in my creative-writing class, demonstrating unreasonably impressive potential from the start; at twenty-five, starting to make short films, her affinity for the visual upstaging her interest in words alone; by thirty, a nationally recognized award-winner for *Speaking in Tongues*, a thirty-minute *tour de force*; and now, several shorter films later, she's ready to direct her first feature-length project. One of the rare delights of teaching, to see an ex-student blossom so exuberantly.

"Are you paying attention?"

"Yes, of course. Why do you ask?"

"Looked like you were zoning out there for a minute."

"I'm hanging on every word."

"Good. Okay, so there's this German thing. It was said that, at some point in medieval Germany, the people were so honest and upright and generally good that a virgin, a *naked* virgin could carry a bag of gold across the country, and she and the gold would arrive safely at the other side. Nobody would touch either one of them."

She looks at me, beaming the faintest note of defiance, as though challenging me to say there is no such story.

"I think I've read something like that."

"So Aaron, I mean Aaron's *character*, is obsessed with this image, except that he wants to transpose it to Newfoundland and make it the basis for his novel. Because he thinks it says something profound about the character of Newfoundlanders, see. Only he can't figure out how to do it. So he imagines all these possibilities—different times in history, different locations, I mean walking all the way across Newfoundland would be a bit much, right?"

"So this has to be magic realism."

"Right, well he's not sure what it will be, I mean there can be animated sections of his fantasies, some can be more realistic, and of course there'll be a lot about what's going on in his own life, troubles with his girlfriend, maybe a love triangle. But the book he's writing, yeah, that could be magic realism. So what do you think so far?"

I'm a bit appalled, actually. The notion of trumpeting the glories of some essentialist version of Newfoundland character seems repugnant, anti-artistic, reductively political. It's a long way from the delicacy of *Speaking in Tongues*, with its original-seeming exploration of those universal chestnuts, communication, love, and creativity.

"Well, this idea of Newfoundlanders as intrinsically honest and so forth seems a little, well, cornball. I mean can it really be the case that Newfoundlanders, as a group, are morally superior to other people?"

"Of course," she says, "it's a ridiculous idea if that's as far as it goes. But see, it's the one he starts with. And there are maybe half a dozen of these attempts on his part to imagine how the idea would work out, but every time the logic of his story leads him to know that things are more complicated, people are more complicated, despite the power of the image he starts with."

"That sounds more promising."

"See, it'll have postmodern ambiguity, a bunch of different plotlines—and a lot of nudity. So people can take from it what they like. And I figure the male critics will be onside because of the nudity. Assuming the virgin is really hot."

"And you want Aaron for the lead?"

"Yeah, he'd be perfect. This guy is confused a lot of the time, and he has these daydream fantasies about the virgin, so Aaron would be excellent."

I know Aaron Spracklin slightly. Four years ago I met him through Raissa. At one point he was going to set up a meeting between me and the mysterious Father Alphonsus Cleary (or at least the man who had been Father Alphonsus Cleary), my then-research interest. Long absent from Newfoundland, Cleary had faked his suicide in 1984 and returned to live in St. John's, adopting a new identity, though almost no one, including me, knew this. His four unread novels had for some time provided useful grist for my scholarly publication mill, but during a conversation with Raissa and Aaron, it became clear that Aaron knew Cleary in his new incarnation. But he wouldn't reveal anything about him, having been sworn to secrecy, and the meeting that he promised to arrange came to nothing—instead of Cleary, it was Aaron who showed up to explain that Cleary wouldn't meet with me after all.

Back then, Aaron was the lead singer in a band called The Zulu Tostoys, and an actor in many local productions including Raissa's *Speaking in Tongues*. Since then he's moved to Toronto, where his acting career has taken off. He's currently doing a one-man show he wrote himself, *A Man Alone in a Room*, characterized, according to the *Globe & Mail* review, by its "dry, self-deprecating wit whose real target is the audience's comfortable assumptions and beliefs."

"So you think Aaron personifies confusion and living through daydreams."

"Well, let's just say those states are not unknown to him. You know, I wouldn't mind playing the virgin myself. But I'm way too old. But. I've got this great ending in mind. Aaron and his girlfriend make up in the end and he persuades her to walk naked through the streets of St. John's carrying a sack of something. God knows how he gets her to do it, I'll have to work that out. Anyway, she agrees to do it on one condition, that Aaron will get naked and go with her. So the last sequence will be the two of them walking along Duckworth past the courthouse or maybe along Military Road in front of the Basilica, with people either gawking at them or ignoring them. I haven't figured that out yet. Or maybe there won't be any other people around. What do you think?"

"It would be...original."

"I figure nudity is always a major hook."

Back home, I sit at the computer and plunge in. *Dear Arlene... sympathy...condolences...you and the children...thoughts have been with you...independent, brilliant, uncompromising spirit...last twenty years, what can I say...remembering the good times we all shared...if there's anything I can do...*

"Lame" is the word that comes to mind. Better than nothing, but just barely.

I think of the last article that Cliff tried to publish, when he'd pretty much decided to give up the quest for a tenure-track university job and retrain to get into IT so he could support his family. The subject was offbeat: the use of imaginary place names in Canadian literature. Cliff had some theory about them, which I've now forgotten, though I remember the title: "From Mariposa to Manawaka and Back: The Road to Nowhere."

The journal he sent it to rejected it on the grounds that the topic was too highly specialized, by which the editor meant "too trivial," but I suspect the real reason was that Cliff had for once allowed his sardonic wit to infiltrate his academic prose. There were several nasty shots taken at some of the more eminent names in CanLit criticism, the people who, despite his scholarly productivity, could find no permanent place for him in the classrooms they controlled. He didn't bother to send the article out again. His swan song, decades premature.

SIX

A rlene MacIntyre has emailed back, a gracious note absolving me of guilt for having abandoned her and Cliff for so many years (and after all, he didn't make an effort either, something I was tactful enough not to point out in my own message) and declaring herself glad to be back in touch now.

And yes, there is something I could do for her. There's going to be a memorial gathering for Cliff in about ten days, nothing churchy, in fact it's going to be at a jazz club, and people are going to make little speeches about Cliff, some who knew him as an academic, others who knew him as a computer guy. But really nobody who knew him when he was a teenager or younger. Maybe I could supply a brief reminiscence that someone could read....

A jazz club?

Arlene has sent as an attachment the draft of a contribution that one of Cliff's co-workers will be making. Rob

Samuelson focuses on Cliff's success as a member of Pacific Northern Insurance's crack IT team ("from the early days of the Producer system, the Billpayer program, all through the Signassure conversion and, most recently, the PayVantage program—in fact, any program where the accounting component was impacted") and on his inscrutability as a human being ("I don't think many got to know him well personally"). But there are also positive comments about his character ("conscientious, almost to a fault...meticulous"), and his "dry sense of humour," and his ability to "stand up for what he believed in."

This last phrase gives me pause. The notion of "what he believed in" as applied to the political infighting at Pacific Northern Insurance seems absurd. What a waste of energy and talent. And yet who is to say what constitutes waste in the overall context of a person's life? Perhaps he was dedicated to his work, perhaps he found it as absorbing and challenging as he would have found a career in academe, maybe more so. Who knows how many lives he "impacted" beneficially?

And yet. "The PayVantage program"? The "Signassure conversion"?

I think back to 1959, when Cliff, Rex Nairn, and I decided, pretty much simultaneously, to become poets. We had a fully formed Romantic sense of the calling. Easy to scoff at it now. We each had our tutelary spirit. Mine was Dylan Thomas, inspired by the poems on the flip side of the family "A Child's Christmas in Wales" LP, especially "In the White Giant's Thigh," whose gorgeous intensity lured me into a world where joy and sorrow, life and death seemed uncannily and wonderfully connected. For Rex, it was Irving

Layton, on the grounds of sexual frankness plus the imagery. For Cliff it was e. e. cummings: he loved the playfulness, the mild rebellion of the fractured syntax. But we all read as much different stuff as we could, critiqued each other's work in a spirit of courteous competitiveness, and in general prepared ourselves for lives dedicated to literary art.

I'll have to tell Rex about Cliff. No one else will. Rex and I exchange one or two emails a year.

Will Cliff's Vancouver audience want to hear about his teenage poeticizing? What would they make of it, anyway? But perhaps it would be new to Arlene. Even back in grad-school days, she complained that Cliff would speak little about his childhood and adolescence.

But probably it's better to go for narrative, some defining anecdote. If I can come up with one.

Maureen left yesterday, and the house has become a mausoleum. Foley, when he's around, senses my depression and stays tactfully distant. It strikes me that getting out would be a good thing to do. It's an overcast humid day, but rain doesn't seem imminent, so I decide to go for a walk.

Long Pond, the unimaginatively named body of water at the northern edge of the campus, seems a good choice, about forty minutes' worth of mild exercise. I stopped running about three years ago (bad knee), and since then I haven't found a substitute for that narrowly focused parallel universe where running takes place. Walking is not so much like leaving your life behind for a time.

I pull into the Fluvarium parking lot. (The Fluvarium: a sort of nature museum whose main feature is a glass wall in the lower level through which you can observe what's going on beneath the surface of a real stream. Hence the pretentious Latinate title.) Half a dozen other cars, old folks (like me!) out for a brief hike, people walking their dogs, a jogger or two, the usual weekday afternoon assortment, I'm assuming. I head for the path leading to the wooden steps that in turn lead to the trail that goes around the pond, a trail that, as I perambulate clockwise, soon morphs into a sidewalk on the bridge at the east end where traffic whizzes past, from behind, disquietingly close.

Safe on the other side, I focus on my current scholarly conundrum: is it too late to begin work on a monograph that would constitute my graceful critical *adieu* to the world of academic publishing? Will I have the time? More important, will I have the energy, the desire, the internal wherewithal to see such a project through? In three years.

Not that I've been idle. In addition to a handful of reviews (see: *A Safe Place*), I've been plugging away at a couple of articles on the latest in a long series of good but neglected Canadian fiction writers who have provided the cannon fodder (or as Lister Craddock would no doubt put it, "can(n)on fodder") for my standing army of publications.

There are more of these good neglected writers than you might think. The defining criteria: male, heterosexual, white (English, Irish, Scottish, or Jewish ethnicity), urban (Toronto or Vancouver preferred), born in Canada, middle-class, and (bonus points here) has either lived in another country or sets much of his fiction in another country, or (preferably) both.

No self-respecting academic would waste his time (don't even think about "her" time) on such writers, so I have the field pretty much to myself.

Richard Karp is my guy for now. Completely unknown in Canada, except for a few other writers, none of whom has any interest in publishing scholarly articles. Died a couple of years ago, in the UK, where he'd lived most of his adult life. A Montrealer, born in 1928. Educated at McGill, moved to England in the mid-fifties, never came back except to visit. That, in itself, is almost enough to guarantee pariahdom in the world of Canadian academe. But there's more. He wrote short stories, not novels, mostly set in England or Europe, though some in the Canada of his youth and early adulthood. Reviewers of the three volumes that Karp published during his first ten years abroad tended to be puzzled and irritated by what they read. "Little seems to happen in these bleak little tales," opined one, "and when something does occur, it appears to be utterly inconsequential." But there's something disconcertingly imaginative about Karp's fixation on the mundane, and that quality must have been recognized by the editors of the respectable journals and magazines that published his work.

In 1965 Karp converted to Roman Catholicism, after experiencing some sort of mystical illumination—a move that ensured he would never be taken seriously in Canada. To be a Jewish expatriate was okay (look at Mordecai Richler), but the conversion put Karp, or at least his career, irrevocably beyond the pale. Talk that an edition of his stories would be published by a "major" Canadian firm dried up as soon as word made its way to Toronto. "English-speaking Canadian Catholics don't read, so where would the market be," the would-have-been publisher wrote to Karp. "At least Jews like books."

Undaunted, Karp continued to write his stories, though now, in one sense, even *less* seemed to happen in them than in the pre-conversion work, though much more was now going on with the language, as Karp began to integrate his newfound sacramental sensibility with his previous dedication to the austerity of the commonplace. He kept publishing in the UK, though as time went on he depended more and more heavily on his wife's income as a secondary school teacher to support his writing.

His one Canadian fan, the eternally marginalized Tom Wetmore of Muskrat Press of Ottawa, himself a transplanted Brit, did bring out a small *Selected* edition of Karp in the mid-seventies, but few took any notice—a not unusual response to Wetmore's productions. (Wetmore also published the novels of Alphonsus Cleary, one of my other recent enthusiasms.) One story in the *Selected* did manage to make an impact, though, when it was anthologized in a classroom-friendly collection of Canadian short fiction.

"Making Solid Contact," atypically set in Canada, is a story about a father trying to teach his young son how to hit a baseball. The father finds, frustratingly, that he himself has difficulty throwing strikes from the mound at the empty Little League field that they're using. His frustration extends to other aspects of his life, we're given to understand in flashbacks: his job, his marriage, his very sense of self are all characterized by varieties of dissatisfaction. But the main narrative issue is his son's struggle to swing the bat properly. The father can guide his son through the appropriate movements with both of their pairs of hands on the bat at once. He can take the bat himself and demonstrate good technique. But left to his own devices, the son tends to hack stiffly at the ball, producing feeble grounders or pop-ups at best. Finally the father gives up and concentrates on simply throwing the ball over the plate. And at last the son "gets it," his swing becomes fluid if not graceful, and in the story's climactic moment, hits a fly ball to left field. At the zenith of the arc of its flight, the father suddenly feels renewed in spirit, as the ball "like a white bird began its ineluctable descent."

The Trinitarian symbolism was overlooked by reviewers, who instead saw the story as an interesting contribution to Canadian sports literature, though one commentator thought the same idea would have "been developed more fittingly in a hockey-related context." Wetmore was later to explain the symbolism himself in one of his cranky little essays on the dim-wittedness of Canadian critics.

So as far as most Canadian readers were concerned, "Making Solid Contact" was a one-off, and its author not worthy of further investigation. By the time I got interested, Karp was about seventy-five, with a dozen collections of stories, and a couple of short novels. *Terra incognita* for the worthy mapmakers of the CanLit crit industry, a godsend for yours truly, I've churned out five articles on Karp's work, all of which have been published. (In the journals I submit to, no one cares how obscure the subject matter is.) The question I'm wrestling with now is whether to go the whole hog and try to write a monograph that would provide a comprehensive introduction to his work. I'll just have time to do it before retirement. My legacy project.

A bizarre symbiosis, I'm thinking—as I truck down the path, exposed to the breeze in this open area, university buildings up a slight rise to the left—this conjoining of writer and critic. Karp is dead and in either heaven or oblivion, Jesus to my Paul. What combination of ego and altruism impels me to spread his Word? The Norman letters, indispensable companion to the gospel of Karp. Check out St. Hughie's Letter to the Philistines, wittily lambasting Karp's long-forgotten reviewers for being, you know, philistines.

I'm now walking past the building where they keep the canoes. No one is on the water today, and there's a "Facility Closed" sign on the short dock, perhaps because of the weather. It's now looking as though the rain may start earlier than I'd thought, probably when I'm exactly halfway around with no shelter in sight.

Structuring the Karp monograph would be difficult. Fourteen books, none of which would be familiar to its hypothetical readers. A lot of plot summary (except plot is unimportant), or focus on certain exemplary works in depth and detail? Sanity would suggest the latter course, but the question of what, exactly, would be "exemplary," would be a concern. I turn over a number of possibilities, but nothing definitive emerges.

At the halfway point, just on the other side of a small footbridge over a stream flowing into the pond, I encounter a strange young man walking in my direction. Normally, the people one meets on this trail have a certain middle-class aura; they'll usually smile, nod, possibly share a word or two, no one in a hurry except the runners.

But this guy is different. He looks more like a standard-issue downtown St. John's hard ticket, despite the knapsack—the badass facial expression that proclaims "Don't fuck with me," the tangle of smudgy-looking tattoos winding up both arms, the arrogant stride, the dark clothes. As we pass each other, our eyes meet. I'm not a believer in demonic possession, but there's something unique in my experience about the intensity of the rage and hatred smouldering there. It isn't directed at me in particular. It has, I'm certain, been there before we met and will continue long after this moment, an ongoing passionately negative judgment on the world as we know it.

I glance over my shoulder and see him moving off the main path, in the direction of the university parking lots and buildings.

Only then do I allow myself to consider how smug my own negative judgment of him has been. Yep, he's evil. Case closed. No need for further analysis. Shame on me, I'm supposed to think.

Still. Those eyes were disturbing.

I'm unsettled enough to forget about the Karp project for the moment. What was he doing here, anyway?

I've come around to the far end of the pond now. The path goes up and down, tall trees on both sides. The foliage is sparse and doesn't start until way up high. The lower trunks seem diseased, barren—though they may exemplify good silviculture practices for all I know. The rain is still holding off. There's a chance I can make it back to the car before it starts.

I seem to have the trail to myself. Young Goodman Brown before he meets the old guy in the forest. Not-so-young and not-so-good, for that matter. And Faith, with her pink ribbons, has headed off to Saskatchewan this week. Returning home, I'd find Terry Foley and his six-pack of Old Stock, temporary keeper of the domestic hearth.

Or—and this is a bit weird—suppose that "returning home" meant dropping in on Andy. Maybe Foley won't be there, so I'll go next door and ring Andy's bell. He'll be welcoming, I'm sure, although, now that I think about it, I've never actually been inside his house, as Maureen and I have become quite ingenious at manufacturing excuses to fend off his incessant invitations. But suppose I *did* come back from Hawthorne's metaphorical forest, world-view and sense of self in ruins. Surely Andy would take me in, offer some non-judgmental reassurance, perhaps provide a reminiscence or two about his own, similar experiences. Or maybe he wouldn't have a clue what I'd be talking about, would look puzzled. A slight squint, possibly, a minor, unnatural-looking twitch involving the right side of his nose, a gesture that might be misconstrued as skeptical by someone who didn't know Andy as well as I, in this pointless fantasy, appear to. And I would tell him the story, twice, three times, until I could see he finally understood. And that would, for some reason, be a deeply satisfying experience.

Fifteen minutes later I'm in the home stretch, the top floor of the Fluvarium looming over the trees at ten o'clock. Time perhaps to revisit the idea of a defining anecdote for Cliff.

I remember his giving a conference paper, around 1980, Edmonton, I think. It was one of our rare get-togethers after grad school, as we scrambled to keep afloat by teaching as sessionals wherever the jobs were, attending conferences on the improbable chance that someone would be impressed enough to offer the chance to be interviewed for a real job.

Back then, Hayden White's *Tropics of Discourse* was a hot new critical book. People looking for instant article and conference paper ideas used it as an advanced version of *Coles Notes*. Cliff found some way to connect one of its ideas to a bunch of prairie novels, but he presented his paper at a session with another White enthusiast, younger than Cliff, a guy with a puppydog eagerness to be hipper-than-thou (in an intellectually cutting-edge way, of course).

I cringed when it became obvious early on, as the other guy delivered his goods, that Cliff would be overmatched on the basis of vocabulary alone. (Cliff valued clarity above all else, against the obscurantist grain of the times.) But when he started to read his own paper, another problem became evident. He was pronouncing White's first name as "Haydn," like the composer, and compounded the problem (literally!) by continuing to use both first and last names as though hyphenation were involved, as in "Haydn-White." After this had happened several times, the chair of the session intervened to suggest tactfully that perhaps the correct punctuation was "Hayden." Cliff paused for only a moment, did not acknowledge the suggestion, and plunged back into his argument. Within two sentences there was another "Haydn-White," and then another. By this time the audience (all seventeen or so of us) was focusing not on the content of the paper—prairie novels, who really cared—but on when the next mispronunciation was coming.

The anecdote would be "defining" because of its ambiguity: was Cliff being stubborn or did he simply not assimilate what was being said to him? Both seemed equally possible, and both were perhaps alternate versions of the same phenomenon. More important, why the mispronunciation in the first place? That was all too obvious, to me anyway. Cliff would have discovered the White book on his own, would not have discussed it with anyone at all, would barely have taken note of the author's name, especially the first one, and would have come to the conference believing such matters to be irrelevant to his main purpose: to apply one of White's ideas to the work of certain prairie novelists, thus making a minor but significant contribution to scholarly knowledge, and, ideally, impressing one or two influential members of the audience with his brilliance.

Cliff at his awkward finest. When we talked afterward, he argued that "Haydn" was a reasonable pronunciation, regardless of what everyone else believed. What did they know? The important thing was the validity of the substance of his argument, wasn't it?

Within a few months the other presenter had been hired for a tenure-track position for which Cliff had also applied. In a letter he noted, aggrievedly, that, in our discipline, "personality" had become more important than "solid achievement."

I play with the notion of massaging this material into the sort of thing that Arlene is looking for, but I know in my heart it's a lost cause. Of course she wants the truth, but not this kind, a kind that she's doubtless all too familiar with.

I'm now almost at the small bridge over Leary's Brook, the stream whose depths you can peer directly into through the glass wall in the Fluvarium's lower level. Straight ahead and up a hill, the parking lot awaits. But, atypically, I'm not ready to pack it in just yet. So—despite the darkening sky—I follow a path away from the main trail into an area of relative wilderness, vestigial side paths indicating that people have lived and worked here before the park existed. I know this place from having been on outings with my grandchildren, who liked to explore what they called "the deep dark forest," enjoying the illusion of being far from civilization.

Another Cliff anecdote. Northrop Frye, Canada's only literary scholar of genius, gives a lecture at UBC. The auditorium is packed. After he finishes—low-key, self-deprecating, quietly witty delivery—questions are invited. The first three or four bear directly on the topic of the lecture. There's a pause. Cliff waves his hand, stands up, is recognized. "Why," he wants to know, "are no courses in Canadian literature offered at the University of Toronto?" (That of course being Frye's home institution.) A hush, a universal sense that this question is in bad taste, awkwardly confrontational as it is. Only someone with my detailed knowledge of Cliff's psyche could register it as rooted in a simple desire to know the answer. Frye is unfazed. "No professor there wishes to teach such a course." What a slimy cop-out, I think. Go get him, Cliff. Follow up. Why don't they *hire* someone who "wishes to teach such a course?" But Cliff merely nods and sits down. It's not clear from his expression whether he's being sincerely deferential or scornfully rejecting the notion that further dialogue is warranted. Someone asks another question, and the matter appears to be forgotten, though Cliff has no doubt been identified as a troublemaker by certainly important figures in the department, something that may affect, however subtly, the quality of the letters of reference he will need.

No, this one won't do either. We need something softer-edged, something more obviously flattering.

It's starting to rain, very gently. I'm following one of the old trails, sloping upward, the smell of the woods mildly intoxicating.

Probably I should go back farther for Cliff material. High school or before. He left Ottawa after grade eleven when his father (perhaps an outsider like his son, having annoyed someone at a higher level of the civil service) moved his family to a small community in northern Ontario where he taught high school, something for which he seemed spectacularly unsuited, shyness or standoffishness his most prominent character trait, probably the former.

I'm paying close attention to the ground. Tree roots, rocks, moss where there's shade, grass in the occasional clearing. Rotting lengths of wood in the swampy parts, once a thoroughfare for horse-drawn carts, I'm guessing, possibly hauling logs. (I prefer not to know the details—the whiff of some semi-imaginary past is what intrigues me.) The diseased-tree motif makes itself evident as well. Whether coniferous or deciduous, they're mostly barren of foliage until well over my head, and some are obviously defunct, many wreathed in what looks like some brittle gray malignancy.

Out of the corner of my eye I notice a shape that doesn't belong. It's on the ground, lumpish. Not a boulder. Not a couple of large garbage bags. I have to push aside a couple of bare branches to get closer, not really believing what I know I'm seeing.

But yes. It's a human being all right, male, face down, and judging from the bloody orifice in the rear left region of the head, a dead one.

My first dead body, corpse, stiff. How can I have lived this long and never seen one?

There's something impressive about its deadness, an aura that approximates the sacred, something transcending the physical specifics: the balding head, for example, with its sadly graying, truncated ponytail. Grayed, one would have to say now. It's something about the stillness, the inertia of rocks and hills, the sense of a final condition achieved. Perfection, of a sort.

SEVEN

My old friend dies, I'm getting mildly obsessed with my own death, and now here's a dead body.

Why does life so often imitate bad art?

If this were a novel, this scene would be the prologue, followed by two hundred pages of flashback.

But that doesn't make it any less real, this body which has now become the centre of my known universe.

Am I in danger? There's no sign of movement in my field of vision, no human-produced sound registering, not that either of those facts means anything.

I take a couple of steps toward the body, but something tells me not to go nearer. "Something tells me?" What would that be, exactly? Okay: I realize I'm not supposed to go nearer. Not a matter of fear, surely? Maybe more like reverence. But what would going nearer accomplish, anyway? I'm not about to roll it over, am I?

And then common sense kicks in: the issue of not disturbing evidence, the prudent response fostered by innumerable cop shows. This must be what it's like to be one of those anonymous characters at the beginning of an episode of *Law and Order*, self-absorbedly going about their business until they stumble upon the corpse. (Cut to the detectives making wiseass comments about the "vic," and then the theme.) Such characters are often questioned briefly by the detectives, I recall. How will I explain what I'm doing here?

The rain is falling harder now. I'll be soaked by the time—less than five minutes if I hustle—it'll take me to get to the Fluvarium. Card-carrying technophobe that I am, I have no cellphone.

Though what's the hurry? No matter how fast I move, there'll be no resurrection. And perhaps I could slink off unnoticed. A tempting thought, but what if I'm seen? That could turn into more trouble. Plus it would be antisocial, irresponsible, immoral.

I think for some reason of the poster that Maureen and I saw in St. Pierre, the missing woman with the sad, beautiful face.

I haven't moved yet. And what sort of movement would be appropriate? If I go racing away from the scene and someone sees me, could that be interpreted as guilty flight? On the other hand, if I make an effort to walk slowly and casually, would that make it look like I was trying to conceal something?

But it *is* raining. Okay. I'll run. Jog, anyway, but slowly, no sense in exposing my bad knee, the left one, to the possibility of further damage. Anyone would hurry to get out of the rain.

And on the way, inspiration strikes. Suddenly I have the perfect anecdote for Arlene MacIntyre, the one that both shows Cliff in the best possible light and conveys everything essential about him.

In grade eleven it was decreed that a certain day would be "Dress-up Day" at all high schools in Ottawa. Girls were to wear dresses, boys suits and ties. It wasn't clear to me—then or now—what its purpose was. Perhaps it was an experiment in social control. But at whose behest? Was it some Cold War-related government psychological intel project? Would youth be so subject to manipulation by authority figures that they would do something that (a) required a certain amount of effort, and (b) had no discernible desirable practical outcome?

Of course almost everyone at our school went along with it. But not quite. Cliff immediately perceived the totalitarian dimension of the enterprise and balked. (This did not please our friend Rex Nairn, by then a student council rep with ambitions to be next year's Head Boy—though he would eventually decide that being Head Boy would be so uncool as to be not worth pursuing.)

On the day, Cliff wore gray casual pants and a brown sweater, nothing out of the ordinary, but the drab colours made his point. No one gave Cliff a hard time—the ethos of our middle-class suburban school would not have permitted that—but everyone knew what he was up to. Cliff, the unobtrusively independent thinker, rejecting the mob mentality of the time simply by doing what he would normally do anyway.

Although this incident certainly represents Cliff at his most Clifflike, it clearly requires some working up to make it dramatic enough for the memorial. But this is of course the problem with Cliff: the absence of drama. How unfortunate that there was no confrontation with the forces of conformity, no moment at which Cliff made an impassioned speech to explain to his classmates the significance of the gesture or engaged in a fistfight with a well-dressed proto-fascist. As I recall the day, hardly anyone even remarked on Cliff's rebellion. The one exception was our mild-mannered Science teacher, the ironically nicknamed "Tiger" Summers, whose quiet comment was "Stick to your guns, Cliff." Perhaps Tiger had good reason to think of himself as a member of a marginalized minority, but no one thought in those terms back then.

I'm wondering if it would be okay to reshape this material somewhat, to supply the climax that the narrative requires. Of course that would be false to my sense of what Cliff was really about, but is that of paramount importance? Maybe the truth would be appropriate for Arlene, but what about the audience of (to me) faceless strangers at the memorial? A difficult ethical issue, I think, as I almost trip over a tangle of tree roots.

Soon I'm back on the main path, taking a sharp left, puffing across the small bridge, then up the ridiculously steep paved walk toward the parking lot, and left again into the Fluvarium, where I can begin to do my duty as a citizen.

It's early evening, the rain has let up, Foley is lounging about the kitchen with a hangdog look as I start to prepare my dinner. At first I think it's because he wants more details on my discovery of the body and my subsequent interview with the police. I've given him only a very brief account, a fact which may have offended him, mostly because I feel drained. But then I realize he's up to something else. He mutters something about having "forgotten to replenish my cache of comestibles" while eyeing the steaks I've taken out of one of my Sobeys bags. (They were on special; I thought I'd freeze the second one.) I break down and ask him to join me.

"You're very kind," he says, using the over-solemn, laying-it-on-too-thick tone that sounds sarcastic but isn't really. "I'll reciprocate in the near future."

"I'll hold my breath."

His expression suggests he's been unjustly insulted, but he says nothing. He'll show me. Or not.

"So it must have been quite a shock."

"Yes, Foley, it was. As I've mentioned."

"You were somewhat laconic on the subject."

"You could make yourself useful by washing the lettuce."

"Certainly. Any idea who this fellow was?"

"No. It never came up. I'd rather not talk about this right now." But who was he, I'm thinking. Who the hell was he?

"Understood," Foley says. He hesitates. "If you need some form of distraction this evening, I have a rough, very rough draft of a piece of writing. Perhaps you could peruse it and offer suggestions? It's quite brief."

"What's it about?"

He looks somewhat abashed. "Birth."

"I beg your pardon?"

"Birth. I'm writing about birth. It's for an anthology. Men's accounts of the birth of their children. $500 for 2,000 words."

"So how did you get invited?"

"A member of the local writing community set it up. One evening I was waxing eloquent about the birth of my firstborn. Your grandson. Over cups. This was some time ago, but she was impressed enough to remember."

"She?"

"The member of the local writing community. She has Toronto connections. This is for a major publisher, you see. Hence the unseemly fee."

"She."

"It wasn't like that, I assure you. It was a genuine spontaneous outpouring of emotion as we compared experiences. There was no ulterior motive."

"'Over cups.'"

"You're suggesting it takes alcohol on top of a disingenuous display of male sensitivity for me to achieve success with a woman."

"But then I'm cynical. So who is it?"

He flashes a look that somehow combines irritation and amusement.

"Can't tell you, old boy. She's married. Not that I don't trust you, but...it was some time ago, in any case."

"Another country."

He doesn't pick up on it. He looks at me, bushy eyebrows raised as though in a self-conscious clichéd signal of surprise. He knows that I know he's never been out of this country.

"Literary allusion. Eliot used it in an epigraph. *The Jew of Malta*."

Dawn breaks. He's recalling a previous incarnation. "'And besides, the wench is dead,'" he says, pleased with himself.

"Only she isn't. Not in another country, either."

There's work to be done, books to be read and reviewed, articles to be written. "The Transubstantiation Motif in the Later Fiction of Richard Karp," fifteen pages of commentary on three stories almost no one but me has ever read, the approach so outdatedly unhip, so two-academic-generations ago, as to make it unpublishable in any self-respecting state-of-the-art journal, lies on my desk, ready to be ruthlessly cut and revised. It's paperweighted by a new anthology of Canadian short fiction the publisher has overly optimistically sent me in the hope that I'll put it on a syllabus. I flip through to the one story (out of forty-three) by a Newfoundland writer. The italicized introductory blurb alerts the reader to be on the lookout for slyly inserted literary allusions. "For example," the editors write, "the cab company takes its name from *Gulliver's Travels*."

I'm tempted to take a few minutes to write to explain to them that in real-life St. John's there is a cab company named Gulliver's, but it has nothing to do with the Swift novel. It has rather to do with the fact that there are people in Newfoundland named Gulliver. Perhaps I should compose a witty letter to the publisher, copied to the editors, or vice-versa, complaining about the ignorance of mainlanders, not caring how self-righteous I might sound, even as I imagine the bored, dismissive response I'd get, if any. *In any future edition we will fully acknowledge the happy coincidence of literary allusion with social reality. Make no mistake, though. We don't really care about this. We can't hope to sell more than a handful of books in Newfoundland, anyway. No one else will notice. And by the way, what species of jerk wastes his time complaining about something this trivial? Please don't bother answering.*

No, I'd better forget such self-indulgence. Instead I set to work on my fictional version of Cliff. Cliff as Horatius at the Bridge, almost the only person in the school to stand up for the right of the individual to rebel against the...well, against what, exactly? The mindless conformity of the fifties? (This would have been 1961.) The dead hand of authoritarian bureaucracy and its subaltern lackeys? All of those forces that would quench the blessed orneriness of the human spirit? As I ponder the ways to shape this narrative, I come to the conclusion that these forces will have to be personified, and the best candidate for that role is our friend Rex Nairn.

But the logic of narrative demands something else. I decide to arrange for a confrontation in the cafeteria, with Rex coming in, his body language threatening physical violence against Cliff (this would never have happened), who responds with an understated, to-the-point speech that causes Rex to back down shamefacedly and draws loud applause from his audience of fifty or so fellow students, who, in my fantasy, are reduced to pin-drop silence from the moment of Cliff's eloquent yet restrained opening sentence, which I may or may not work up the nerve to compose. "That moment," I'll conclude, "defined the essential Cliff MacIntyre."

I decide not to send the piece off to Arlene immediately. I have the feeling it won't look quite so impressive in twenty-four hours.

Then I send Rex a brief email summarizing the facts that Arlene has provided. I don't tell him about the memorial gathering and my contribution to it, lest he want to see what I've written and (worse) write something himself.

Dinner over, Foley gone out, the doorbell rings. Andy, insisting I come over for a beer. Thinking I might as well get it over with, plus I can use a distraction from the unsettling events of the afternoon, I agree to join him on his small back deck.

I resolve not to tell him about finding the corpse. We'll keep this light. No death today. When I've recalled telling him about Cliff, I've felt almost as though I've betrayed Cliff somehow, though that idea makes no sense.

After the initial exchange of pleasantries, we sit in uneasy silence, looking across the fence separating my yard from his. Good fences make good neighbours, I nearly say, but then realize I'd have to try to explain the Frost poem to him, and in the end he'd only look baffled. And in those terms, he wouldn't be pro-fence anyway, I don't think.

Someone close by is barbecuing. There's the noise of kids playing. A dog barks, then three more dogs, farther away. Life is proceeding as normal, except here on Andy's deck. Why has he called this meeting?

"You know," he says (always in my experience a warning sign; almost never do I "know" what the person speaking to me alleges that I know), but then he stops. "Well, maybe you don't know"—can he read my mind?—"but your friendship, yours and Maureen's, has meant a lot to me over these past few months."

Friendship? He's got to be kidding. I decide to keep quiet, lest I say something unfortunate.

"You've been such great neighbours. And I think I've mentioned that my girlfriend's coming to visit soon." He's making sure we've got eye contact. Is this where he tells me his girlfriend is really a guy? (Not that there's anything wrong with that.)

"And I'm hoping that she and you guys will really hit it off."
She. Okay, but why wouldn't we?

"Well, I'm sure we will," I've decided to say. "When does she arrive?"

"Tomorrow. But here's the thing." Andy seems suddenly shy, totally out of character. He looks away, into my backyard, possibly at the moss on the shed roof. "Sometimes people find her...a bit much."

He's still looking away. "She has some...odd ideas. Or people find them odd. Her research...well, I just thought I'd better give you a heads-up." He holds his hand up, anticipating my question. "I won't say more now. "

"Okay then, forewarned is forearmed. As it were. Too bad Maureen is out of town at the moment. How long will she be staying, your girlfriend?"

"Cynthia," he says. And I'm all ready for him to say, with theatrical deliberation, "Her name is Cynthia," but he doesn't. Nor does he answer my question. Instead he turns back to me and declares: "I'm deeply in love with her."

Deeply in love. Do people of his generation, *men* of his generation, actually say stuff like that? I'll check with Foley, but I'm pretty sure they don't. I'm betting Andy is a one-off.

It was on a bright and windy afternoon in April 1995 [Foley's essay begins], *a few days after the Oklahoma City bombing, that my firstborn entered the world. As the McMurrough Federal Building lay in ruins, already the spin doctors of the right were using the event to foster racial hatred. (Remember the canard about unidentified Middle Eastern men wearing the clothing unique to their culture supposedly seen acting suspiciously before and after?) A world of deception and mendacity. Of course the perpetrator was eventually revealed to be a proto-fascist zealot, a marginalized member of the American working class, product of a system that privileges sociopathic behaviour as the means to personal and collective achievement.*

Into such a world was Ryan Michael Foley born.

At this point I stop reading.

Bizarrely, I feel the need to call Sandra.

I try the cottage country number and in seconds, she's there, sounding just a tad blurry. Apparently in Ontario the sun has sunk below the yardarm some time ago.

There's a moment of hesitation when she recognizes my voice, a kind of muted exasperation as she pronounces my name, as though I'm responsible for reducing the effect of her g-and-t by about thirty percent. "What is it about?" Cordially delivered but the tone says I'd better have a good reason. "Is it Cliff MacIntyre?"

"No, it's not about Cliff."

"Did Arlene get in touch with you eventually? Or you with her?"

"Yes. Yes she did. But that's not why I'm calling."

"Oh." The intonation here means that since Cliff's death provides the only conceivable reason that we might be communicating with each other at this post-historical juncture of our relationship, she now expects to be told something that right this second is, to her, in the realm of the unimaginable.

"I was thinking of the day Ryan was born. Do you remember it?"

"Ryan?" Now the tone implies that she has memories of thousands of individual births, and conjuring up the one appropriate to that of her first grandchild might be a bit of a strain.

"Yes, Ryan. Your first grandchild?"

That was a mistake.

"I know who Ryan is. Are you drunk again?"

Again. I love it, in one sense. More evidence that we've been divinely sanctioned not to be together.

"I don't think so." I'm trying to give the impression that I'm a reasonable guy, open to being persuaded that he's wrong.

"What is it that you want to know, then?"

I love her use of "then," too. Very Sandra.

"Well, Terry is writing an essay for an anthology. It's about men's experience of birth, and…"

"*Men's* experience of birth?" The incredulity quotient here suggests Sandra is envisioning essays in which men lie about how babies have popped out of their navels or sprung from their foreheads.

"Yes, about the experience of their partners' giving birth, you see. He's writing about that, and it got me to thinking about what it was like when Ryan was born, what it was like for us, I mean. What you felt at the time. What it was like for you to think that here it was, a new generation that was connected to us. Sort of thing." I consider pausing here but realize I can't. I have to keep going, even as my voice indicates I'm losing confidence by the second, that I think what I'm saying is ridiculously lame even as I also recognize it's the truth. "You know, we'd been split up for years, but you came back here for the birth, and it was like the fact that we'd once been together was even more important than it was because we produced Emily, because now we'd sort of produced another generation, by proxy, as it were. Without us there wouldn't have been Emily and without Emily there wouldn't have been Ryan. I don't think this is making much sense, is it?"

Finally I do stop. So this is why I've called her. Cliff has died. I've just seen my first corpse. I need to be connected to someone who can tell me that my life has had some point, and she's the only candidate I can come up with. Maureen hasn't been around long enough. Foley, of course, hardly counts.

I remember what it was like when she stayed with me at my (formerly our) house when Ryan was born, there being not enough room in Emily and Foley's tiny rented row house in Georgestown (and me, fortuitously, living alone at the time). How decorous we were, how careful about not revealing inappropriate body parts, how solicitous about pandering to each other's near-forgotten domestic foibles. Yet there was something chastely conspiratorial about our being together, as though the advent of Ryan was something we had cooked up, though our vital role could not be publicly acknowledged. Or so I thought.

"You're saying," Sandra is now saying, "that the birth of Ryan sort of made us immortal, as a couple? Or you as an individual? Is that what you're concerned about?"

"I don't know that I'm 'concerned' about anything." (Yes I am.) "I hadn't thought about immortality." (No, just about its opposite.)

Sandra makes an ingressive whooping noise meant to connote mirthful derision. "It's a very sentimental view of it all, isn't it? I just remember it was a lot of hard work, helping Emily to cope, with little tangible support from her ne'er-do-well husband."

When was the last time anyone used the term "ne'er-do-well" in conversation?

"I remember," she says, starting to get into it now, "there was that flaky woman doctor with the coloured hair. There was Foley sleeping in when Emily's water broke. Ten in the morning and he had to be hauled out of bed, kicking and screaming. And you had to drive them to the hospital because Foley of course couldn't drive, let alone afford a car. And then the struggle Emily had getting Ryan to latch. God, what agony. For everyone. For days. Poor thing. And when she was in labour they wouldn't give her that drug, what is it, because of the timing."

"An epidural?"

"Yes. It was too late, that doctor said. With the sparkly rainbow junk in her hair. But this isn't what you want to hear, is it?"

"It's not a question of want. I was just curious about your, er, perspective."

"Well. Did I think our destiny was to be revered as founders of a line of heroic leaders and Nobel Laureates? No, not when Terry Foley is part of the genetic mix."

"I take your point. But that wasn't quite what I had in mind."

"No. I know it wasn't. Hugh, are you all right? Is this anything to do with what's-her-face?"

I should have seen that one coming.

"No." I refrain from pointing out that Maureen and I have been together for four years, and that Sandra knows what her name is.

"No?"

"Be assured that this is something quite separate from anything having to do with what's-her-face."

"Is it Cliff's death that's upset you, then?"

"I don't think I'm 'upset,' but it has been a shock, yes."

"I see," Sandra says, as though my response has revealed such deep and complex deficiencies in my psyche that it would be injudicious of her to say more without due deliberation. "Well, Keith is trying to get my attention. I think I'd better go now."

I turn back to Foley's manuscript, flipping through at random.

The contractions kept coming. Emily kept pushing. Not for nothing is it called 'labour,' I thought, hard work in the service of the life-force, that silent and invisible Simon Legree that scoffs at our attempts to take job action, let alone unionize. (Though one supposes that contraception would in fact constitute a kind of effective gesture of civil disobedience, it was far too late for that now, Emily having somehow subverted my best efforts in that department, a cause of some acrimony between us in the early stages of her pregnancy.)

Odd how that sort of perception, however valid, vanishes when the moment of truth arrives. Yes, I am conscious of the fact that that phrase is a cliché. Yet what else to call it, when Amanda Cochrane, our doctor, beckons me around to see the top of a tiny head begin to emerge from Emily's vagina. Yes, at that moment we are no longer indentured servants slogging it out on the assembly line of human reproductivity. No, one cherishes, for that nanosecond of consciousness, the illusion that one has contributed to the creation of a fresh and unique manifestation of human nature, that one has triumphed over that which would keep us imprisoned in the roles assigned to us by the tyranny of late capitalism.

"Keep pushing," Amanda Cochrane enjoined Emily. "It's coming," I chimed in, not without a sense of guilt, for what is my role here but something analogous to that of the factory owner who profits from the toils of his employees, as I grin witlessly at the immense return on my investment of a few squirts of semen. Yes, a crass image, I know. But here truth must be privileged and witnessed to, however unsavoury its content. For once I share the mindset of the oppressor, even as I feel pity for the infant, whose assimilation by the rapacious yet seductive forces of consumerism is all but inevitable.

"Can you see it?" Emily asks me, a touching gesture of trust. It is to me that she turns for valid information, not the doctor.

"Yes I can," I tell her. "I can really see it."

EIGHT

"Police are tight-lipped," the voice on the radio is saying, "about the identity of the body found yesterday in a wooded area near the Fluvarium. And they're not saying much about the circumstances of its discovery. Spokesperson Constable Christine Parsons told the news media in a brief press conference this morning only that foul play has not been ruled out. No arrests have been made, she said."

Foley and I are at the kitchen table. He's somewhat morose. I've returned his birth experience manuscript and explained in general terms what I think the problems are. He hasn't taken it well. "I thought a different perspective would be good," he's said. "I mean, how many of these essays are likely to explore the political context of birth? It's going to be all sensitive New Age guys gushing about what a mind-blowing experience to be there when the missus popped. I wanted mine to be different, that's all."

"In that you succeeded."

He hasn't replied to this remark. We're sitting at the kitchen table, sipping our coffee in silence, avoiding eye contact. Five full minutes have passed. But when he hears the news item, he perks up.

"I know you don't want to talk about this yet," he says, "but maybe at some point we could have a chat about your experience yesterday. I think maybe I could write it up and sell it somewhere."

"I'll think about it." I say this to mollify him. I can't imagine ever having such a conversation. He picks up on this immediately.

"I'd frame it appropriately, of course. Nothing to make you look ridiculous or anything. The experience of a representative middle-class liberal who's forced to confront the reality of the violence that lurks just below the surface of his comfortable...well, you know what I mean. Your trauma is perfectly understandable, the result of decades of..."

"Enough, Foley."

"You see, if you'll forgive me, that's precisely the attitude that..."

"Foley. How many corpses have you seen? Shut the fuck up."

Around ten o'clock in the morning, the doorbell rings. I'm upstairs, in my study. Foley answers the door. I hear a man speaking, words indistinguishable, Foley responding, then calling my name.

"This gentleman is from the Constabulary," Foley says in formal, butler-parodying terms as I come down the stairs. "He wishes to have a word with you."

It's not the detective from yesterday. This guy is big, maybe six-three or -four. He's about forty-five, maybe, receding hairline, slightly prominent front teeth, glasses. And he's dressed casually, a hoodie, jeans, sneakers. Is this standard practice?

"Dr. Norman," he bellows. It's not a question. He's telling me who I am. But he's also smiling.

"Yes?"

"Gene Brazil." After almost twenty-five years, I'm still not quite used to the accent on the first syllable of that surname. I wait for him to say something else. "Can I come in, sir." Again it's not really a question. On principle I should tell him No. He has no right to burst in like this. On the other hand, refusal will engender suspicion and, ultimately, no doubt, an encounter in a windowless interrogation room. Foley, of course, will be taking careful note of the fact that I'm willing to watch my civil rights go up in smoke without making a peep. He's retreated down the hallway to Maureen's study, which he's been allowed to use as a workspace in her absence.

Brazil takes note of my hesitation. "It'll take just a few minutes, sir. I was just on my way in to work, passing by, you know, and I saw your car in the drive, so I thought I'd save us both some time. I'd have to call you later anyway, and by then you might be at work yourself."

In my paranoid translation this works out to: "I'm watching your every move. I could haul you in to the station if I wanted to. Everyone knows you profs don't do real work anyway." But maybe I should just take it all at face value. Brazil's friendly seeming smile hasn't gone away. But why is he on his "way in to work" at ten in the morning?

What do I have to fear?

"Sure, no problem," I say. "Come on in to the kitchen. Can I make you a cup of coffee? Or tea?"

"No, no, no thanks," Brazil responds, the tone implying that there's something immoral about the suggestion, that no right-thinking person such as himself could entertain it for a moment. But he follows me into the kitchen, a more appropriate place than the living room, some part of me has decided, to conduct whatever business is to follow.

Brazil's eyes are everywhere, looking for what? Signs of drug use? Yesterday's murder weapon? Something to confirm his well-concealed but no doubt strong suspicions about my relationship with Foley? But he says nothing, pulls out a chair, sits down, extracts a piece of paper from the manila envelope that I haven't noticed until now that he's been carrying.

It's a copy of my statement from yesterday.

Brazil clears his throat. "Your statement," he says. "Not much to it, is there? Wha? *Wha?*" The word "wha" in this context is not really a contraction of "what"—it's more like an intensifier, an attempt to impress the listener with the seriousness and importance of the speaker's claim, and to establish verbal dominance. Brazil has continued to grin, and has now added a sort of interrogative squint, as if to say, "You must surely agree there's more to it than *that*."

What I say is: "I tried to be concise."

"Con*cise*? I guess you succeeded there." I'm somewhat unnerved by this echo of my earlier comment to Foley ("In that you succeeded.") "I'm surprised," he goes on, "that Detective Mercer let you off the hook so easily." What hook, I'm wondering. Mercer was a younger man, and he seemed almost solicitous, concerned perhaps that making such a discovery might have unhinged a geriatric like me. Several times he'd interrupted his questioning to ask how I was doing. Once he even used the phrase "bearing up." Brazil is clearly no such respecter of persons.

"Detective Mercer seemed very professional," I offer. "He did say that someone else from the Constabulary might contact me." But he didn't say "better not leave town while the investigation is going on." Or did he?

Brazil starts to say something, then pauses and starts again. "Well, *I* want a bit more detail."

"You mean about the body? I hardly looked at it."

"No, no sir. Not about the *body*. About how you came to *find* the body in the first place."

I'm feeling increasingly uneasy. Should I call a lawyer? If so, who? I haven't had to deal with a lawyer in years. And anyway, I'm innocent.

"Where do you want me to start?"

"Well, why were you there?"

"Why was I there where I found the body?"

"No sir, before that. Your car was parked in the Fluvarium lot. What were you doing there? Never mind what you told Detective Mercer yesterday. Let's start over today. All right?"

From somewhere Brazil has produced a small notebook and pen. He makes some show of preparing to jot things down, as though he expects me to go into full-blown lecture mode. If he's trying to intimidate me, it's working. But why would he want to do that?

I'm now sitting at the kitchen table, Brazil across from me. I have to look up at him to make eye contact, something he's clearly more comfortable with than I am. An athlete in his youth, almost certainly. Probably now coaches kids' hockey and baseball. Jock culture. Jock values. The sort of man who, on a given day, would think it important that one team of seven-year-olds beats another team of seven-year-olds. Bald on top now, stringy brown hair protruding from behind each ear. Move on, Hughie. This isn't helping.

"I was there just because I wanted to go for a walk."

"This was what, sir, about 2:30?"

"Yes."

"So you were coming from the university, were you?"

"No. From home."

"You weren't at the university at all?"

"No. This is my research semester. I'm not teaching any courses. I work mostly at home."

"You do research at home, do you, sir? What sort of research would that be?" Here he glances around the kitchen, as though the appliances and cupboards might provide some clue about academic interests. Perhaps, he seems to be implying, you're working on a monograph on dishwashers?

"Well, I write articles, book reviews, that sort of thing."

"You're a professor in the English Department, are you, sir?"

How would he know this? I think I did tell the detective yesterday that I teach at the university, but I'm pretty sure I didn't mention the department. Is Brazil yet another former student of mine? They're always popping up, often unrecognizable to me, but in his case I don't think so. So he must have done some research of his own. But why?

"Yes, that's right."

"So in the summer you just stay home and write, do you? What do you write about, if you don't mind my asking?"

"Well, about books."

He thinks this one over. "You *write* about *books*," he says, emphasizing both verb and noun. The notion that such an activity is possible has apparently never before occurred to him. Writing books is one thing, but writing *about* books...? It's a wacky idea, he seems to be thinking, but some of those profs are probably just wacky enough to do it.

"Yes, I write about books."

He stares at me for a moment, his squint now somehow connoting incredulity. Does he expect me to supply him with a list of authors and titles? Apparently not. Nor does he make a show of writing anything in his notebook. The fact is either too trivial or too momentous to require an entry. He sighs, in the manner of someone starting over at square one.

"So you got to the parking lot at the Fluvarium at about 2:30."

"Yes."

"Why did you happen to go there at that particular time of day, sir?"

"No particular reason. I'd been working on something for several hours, and I needed a break." This is of course a lie. I'd wasted most of the day up until then, but it's not really any of his business, is it?

"Did you tell anyone you were going?"

"Only Terry. The guy who let you in." It seems oddly formal to use Foley's first name.

"And he is...your roommate?" Just the hint of a smirk.

"Actually, he's my ex-son-in law. He's staying here for a few days."

"Your *ex*-son-in-law?"

Thought I'd seen it all, Brazil's expression seems to imply, but this is something new.

"Yes." As soon as I've said this, I start having doubts. I can't actually remember telling Foley that I was going for a walk. Had he already gone out himself? Sooner or later, a voice synthesized from a lifetime's worth of watching cop shows is saying in my head, These guys always trip themselves up with their lies. Give them enough rope and they'll hang themselves.

Has Brazil registered that moment of hesitation? And if so, does he attribute it to the fact that I'm lying about Foley?

"So you tell Terry, your ex-son-in-law, that you're going for a walk. You drive to the Fluvarium. You park your car. You start walking... 'clockwise,' I believe you told Detective Mercer, around the pond. Is that accurate?"

"Yes."

"Why clockwise, sir?"

"Why not? It was an arbitrary choice." This is not quite true. I always walk around clockwise because that way I get the relatively unenjoyable part, walking across the bridge with traffic whizzing past, over with. But how can I tell Brazil this? The idea of dividing a walk around the pond into "enjoyable" and "less enjoyable" segments seems pathetic. What sort of person would do that?

"Arbitrary," Brazil says, writing something down. "Okay. So you walk around the pond. See anything unusual?"

"No."

"Not many people, I guess, were there?"

"Very few. It looked like it was about to rain."

"But that didn't concern you."

"No. I thought I could make it all the way around before it started."

"Now you told Detective Mercer that about 3:15, and I'm quoting here, you 'came to a point near the Fluvarium where there's a path that branches off to the left from the main trail.' You followed this path that leads to a wooded area. Why did you do that, sir?"

I have the feeling that another "arbitrary choice" line is somehow not going to cut it, though why should I even worry about that? Nonetheless I do. I decide to go for the truth and see if that sets me free.

"I had something on my mind that I wanted to work out before I went home. An old friend of mine died a few days ago, and his widow asked me to write something to be read at his memorial gathering. So I was thinking about that, about what I should write."

Brazil considers this for a moment. He hasn't become *un*friendly, exactly, but his tone has shifted into something closer to formality. "You could have kept walking on the main trail, though, couldn't you? Why did you turn left?"

"Good question." (Why the hell have I said that? He'll be sure to find it patronizing.) "Well, I'd been on that path with my grandchildren a few times over the years. But not for a long time now. I guess I thought it would be nice to revisit the place."

"Even though it was about to rain."

"I wasn't too concerned about that. I thought that if it started to rain hard, I could get back to the car in less than five minutes."

"Right." Brazil seems to be humouring me now. "Okay. Then you told Detective Mercer that you walked for about three minutes, you saw an object on the ground, you moved closer and saw it was a man. So you had walked *in*to the woods, looking for what? Why did you decide to go where the body just happened to be?"

"I don't know. I was just kind of wandering around, I guess."

"See, if you'd gone straight ahead with the stream on your right, if you'd kept on that way, you wouldn't have come across it. But you turned to the left. Was that another arbitrary choice?" The grin is back; I'm inferring there's a bit of nastiness to it now.

"Yes."

"Okay. So you see this object that turns out to be a man. Did you recognize him, sir?"

"How could I? He was face down. And sort of turned away from me."

"So that's a no?"

"Yes, it's a no."

"You came within ten feet of him, you said yesterday. You estimated the distance in feet, according to the statement that Detective Mercer took down, not metres. I guess that's a generational thing, would you say, sir? In any case, you got quite close. But you had no idea who he was."

"No."

"No need to raise your voice, sir. I'm right here."

"Sorry." He's looking very pleased at the moment.

"No need to apologize, sir. But I'm just doing my job. Wha? But I'm sure you understand, right? And that's about all I need anyway. For this morning." Now that he's got me rattled, he's ready to return to his earlier, more congenial persona.

As we're shuffling into the porch, I'm half-expecting him to pull a Columbo move, and ask a final, unexpected question prefaced by "I almost forgot," a question that seems irrelevant and trivial but will later prove to be devastatingly incriminating for the smartass criminal who answers it. I brace myself for this.

But all he says is "Thank you for your time."

As I turn away from the door, Foley is ambling out of the back study, where he must have overheard everything.

"It's a bit worrying, isn't it," he says, "given the Constabulary's well-deserved reputation for ineptitude in murder investigations." He's referring to the fact that twice in the not-so-distant past the wrong man was convicted, the injustices reversed only years later.

"Once again Foley demonstrates his mastery of the obvious." (But I'm oddly touched by the fact that he finds the situation "worrying.")

"Sorry. I just meant that perhaps you should consider engaging legal counsel."

"But I'm innocent, Foley. I have faith in the system."

"Ironic to the end. Right in character."

"What do you mean, 'end?'"

Back in my study, I'm feeling both shame and fear in approximately equal intensities, ridiculous emotions both. Why should Gene Brazil have such power? Yet his dissection of my life has revealed to him and vicariously to me how absurd and morally shady an enterprise it is in the eyes of any down-to-earth guy like himself. A man drawing a salary from the public purse who doesn't have to show up at his office, who can sit at home reading books and writing about them at his leisure, who can in the middle of the day take the time to wander aimlessly into the woods like a homeless person drunk on cheap wine. Sixty-two years old, holder of a Ph.D., and this is the best use he can make of his time?

Then there's the fear, even more ludicrous. Is Brazil so desperate that he'd try to frame me? Yes, I discovered the body, but what about motive? What about means? There's no way he could connect me to the murder weapon, should they ever find it. The fact that I'm even driven to think in these terms implies something dark (or at least unflattering) about my grip on reality. I can imagine Brazil reporting to his superior: "I think I like this Norman guy for this one. He's the one turns up the stiff. Probably thinks it's a good cover. Professors think they're smarter than everybody else. But he was nervous, no doubt about that. He's got something to hide, that's for sure. Wha?"

Perhaps getting out of the house will help, but didn't I think that yesterday, and look where it got me. A jaunt to the university is sure to be depressing. A hike around the pond is of course out of the question. ("See, I told you. These guys always return to the scene.")

Then there's the mall.

The parking lot is jammed, as it is whenever I go there, which is not often, and always with some specific purchase in mind. Today, though, I don't mind cruising along the rows of vehicles, waiting for a space to open up, that golden moment when someone pulls out just as I approach. When it finally happens, I go through the entrance by the food court. I'm just beginning to get my bearings when I see someone striding in my direction.

At first he registers as a generalized embodiment of local minor-league hoodlum culture, but quickly morphs into the angry, hate-exuding individual I saw during my walk around the pond yesterday. He glances at me, then away. He has no idea who I am. Then he's out the door.

Can he have been the shooter? Certainly he's the only person I saw who seems a likely candidate. But that in itself means nothing, obviously.

What may mean something is that I didn't mention this guy to Gene Brazil. How will it look if I call him up and do that now? ("So you remember this suspicious-looking character only after we had our little chat, is that right, sir? Some would call that very convenient. Wha? *Wha*?") Yes, Brazil did ask in a general sort of way about whether I saw anyone else on my walk. But I completely forgot about Mr. Don't-fuck-with-me. An honest mistake. Right.

Disoriented, I wonder what this bizarre not-quite-meeting may mean. Probably nothing, is the obvious answer. But there's the nagging possibility that it's part of a larger pattern which, if rightly perceived, would...well, what *would* it do? Provide the sort of aesthetic pleasure that comes from contemplating a work of art, but writ large, very large, since one's life will have been the subject? Show that the apparent randomness of experience is in fact illusory, a revelation that would—or at least could—lead to spiritual illumination, transcendence? Or what?

And how sad a life must that young man be living.

I take the escalator down to the level which houses the chain bookstore, browse for five minutes, and then I realize that there's a way I can infuse significance into this expedition.

It's been at least fifteen years since I last frequented the barbershop here, and yet I'm recognized the instant I step inside. "Haven't seen *you* here for a while," says the man whose name I recall as being something like Gary Butler. In the early nineties he was a slim twenty-something, but now he's gone to seed in a big way, with his florid complexion and bulging gut. Where have I been, he wishes to know. How do I answer that? At a certain point someone suggested I try the Duckworth Street shop run by my ex-student Fred or Wilf, and I came to prefer it, with its retro-cool out-of-the-fifties ambience plus the likelihood of not having to wait if one chose one's times carefully. But I can't say that.

Instead I mumble something about having moved to the east end, as though that would have made it impossible to drive for ten minutes to the barbershop of my choice.

Butler nods, pretending that what I've said makes perfect sense, then asks me what I want done. He's puzzled by the obvious fact that I've recently been to a barber.

"I want the beard off," I tell him. "All of it." How oddly liberating, just to say it. As though I've been using the beard as a mask. The Phantom of the Opera.

"How long've you had it, then?" Butler wants to know. He remembers it from back when.

"Thirty years, give or take."

He makes a sort of clucking sound, which may connote either disapproval or sympathy. I'm not about to ask.

A few months after Sandra and I split up, my hair started to fall out in small, irregular patches. Butler diagnosed it as alopecia, a judgment deemed correct by the mousy-looking young female doctor I subsequently saw at the Health Sciences. She'd feel comfortable giving me steroids for it, she said. Her use of the word "comfortable" seemed absurd. My taking steroids would cause her to experience comfort. I never did fill the prescription she gave me, and shortly afterward my hair began to grow back.

As Butler finishes up—it's taken all of three minutes—I remind him of the alopecia diagnosis and he seems pleased, obviously having wondered if I was going to mention it.

"Yes, I remember that," he tells me.

I overtip him, a ten dollar bill for a service worth six.

"See you again," he says, apparently without irony.

"Absolutely," I reply, in a manner that I hope conveys my new-found resolve to start patronizing the shop again. A female barber, who in the old days would occasionally report that she'd seen me jogging around Quidi Vidi Lake, waves as though it was yesterday.

Driving home along Freshwater, modest houses punctuated by the taxation centre. A Shoppers Drug Mart, a small auto repair shop whose sign advertises its having been founded in 1946, a convenience store with gas pumps, Mary Brown's Fried Chicken, the high school on the right, Booth, in all its self-effacing Salvation Army abstemiousness even if long since de-denominationalized.

Richard Karp would have discovered something here, something denied to me, a hint of divine presence, a sense of the sacred subtly permeating the lives of the (to me) somnambulant denizens of the neighbourhood. Including me, no doubt. The purgatorial removal of the beard reflecting the spiritual transformation that occurs as Gary Butler, that unlikely Virgil, points me in the right direction, facing the mirror. Myself as I really am, barefaced.

But that would be fiction.

"So," Cynthia Tiefenauer is saying, "what's *your* position on UFOs?"

We're sitting on Andy's deck. It's dusk, another pleasant evening when it's possible to believe that, even in St. John's, the livin' is easy, a proposition contradicted by the weather in almost any month but August.

Cynthia is high energy, possibly high maintenance. She's tall and slim, like Andy, long straight blondish hair, brown eyes. But there's something ascetic about her, as though she's made to be a character in a Bergman film, placed in a world of stark, simple architecture in an inhospitable landscape, emotionally distant, possibly suicidal. The woman who denies love to the male protagonist. She's wearing brown shorts and a beige top. Her eyes burn with the no-nonsense light of fanaticism.

But Andy, it's already clear, is besotted. From the introduction half an hour ago until now he's been wearing a goofy smirk, occasionally making eye contact with me in such a way as to say "See? I *am* in a relationship with the most wonderful woman in the world." Sure you are, Andy, my silent response is meant to communicate. Sure you are.

Cynthia's question, bizarre as it sounds, is actually on point. We've established that she's working on her doctorate in Sociology, thesis topic: the alien abduction phenomenon. I've said that that sounds interesting. Now I'm expected to have a "position."

"I haven't really thought that much about it." I know that's not going to be enough.

"But *everyone* has thought about it, right? The culture is saturated with UFO slash alien memes. That can't be an accident." She says this as though I've just said it could be. I look quickly over at Andy. He's enthralled, and I realize it has nothing to do with the content of Cynthia's speech—it's the passion with which she delivers it. And I see too what makes them tick as the improbable couple they are: sometimes that energy is focused on Andy, and it ignites something reciprocal in him, and the Bergmanesque ice lady miraculously vanishes. Or so I imagine. "Take Roswell," she's saying now. "You've heard of Roswell, right?"

"Yes, of course."

"Tell me what you know about Roswell."

"Well, supposedly a flying saucer crashed in New Mexico in 1947, was it, and the military recovered the corpses of a couple of little green men, or something, and—"

"Stop right there. See, that's what they want you to think. It's a hoax. A cover story to preserve some minor military secrets. It was the beginning of the Cold War, right? As for the little green men, the first anyone heard of them was thirty years later. Because it served somebody's interest then to have the population think, at some level, that it's possible that aliens can fly millions of light years across the galaxy only to crash when they get here. How plausible is that?"

"So what's behind it, then?"

I think I see Andy shake his head, almost imperceptibly. But it's too late.

"Well, that's one of the questions I'm trying to address. There's a story that we're meant to buy into, maybe at a subconscious level, or a frivolous suspension-of-disbelief level. But it gets into our heads. And whoever is controlling that narrative has real power."

"Maybe that's enough for Hugh for one night," Andy ventures, but Cynthia's having none of it.

"You're really interested, aren't you, Hugh? You're not just being polite?'

"Certainly not. I'd love to hear about your research."

"Right, well I'm focusing on the abduction phenomenon as a microcosm of the whole problem. Betty and Barney Hill, right? The original abduction story. And yet US military intelligence was involved from day one, and it was only when they were hypnotized that the alien story emerged. Is there evidence these things are happening? It's all anecdotal. Hypnotic regression, very shaky, unscientific, and the big names—Hopkins, Jacobs, Mack—have all been debunked, sorry, you've probably never heard of them, just as well. So what's left? Personal testimony by the so-called abductees who remember without being hypnotized. They're not lying, presumably, but what's that worth? So they're all delusional? Is it mass psychosis? What's going on that makes people imagine that it's happening to them? How do we explain the consistency of their stories?"

She stops for breath. I'm hoping Andy will intervene more decisively to change the subject, but instead he says, "You forgot MILABS."

"Right, MILABS," Cynthia says, gearing up for another round. "Military abductions," she explains, turning back to me. "If some of these experiences are real, I mean objectively real, many, most, or all of them could be our own earthling military doing it for who knows what purpose. American military tech is probably a half century ahead of what the public knows. Maybe it suits the powers that be to spread this meme of aliens are out to get you, keeps the population in fear, distracts people from facing real issues, maybe conditions society to adopt certain attitudes, accept certain ways of thinking. We're powerless, so be afraid. Keeps us wondering if there are dark secrets the government knows and may one day reveal."

"It's like a religion," Andy chimes in, very comfortable now in his role as second banana in this performance.

"It *is* a religion," Cynthia says with some vehemence. "For both conventional religious believers and atheists. One thing is for sure, whether or not any of it is true. If we believe the government knows something we don't, if they seem to do a not-quite-good-enough job of covering it up, they've got us where they want us." She stops and looks at me as if to demand a response.

"Um, I never thought of it that way."

"They don't want you to," Cynthia says. "That's what they don't want."

Maureen is having a wonderful time, she tells me. Exciting new people, great feedback on her poems. I haven't told her about my encounter with the corpse, not wishing to spoil the glow of her enthusiasm with such a blunt-force fact, one that would require a dreary reconfiguring of her emotions. Better to let her enjoy the bubble of good feeling that surrounds her for the moment. As I have enjoyed similar bubbles, both small (my half-hour infatuation with Dr. Sherry Kirsch) and large (my entire professional life, maybe). Of course that may be changing. I don't tell Maureen about the beard, either. She might be alarmed, mildly. I've never in her experience done anything like that before. Instead I tell her about Cynthia and Andy, and how strange it is that they're together, and this of course interests her. And I tell her that Foley has been a model houseguest, and that I really really miss her.

And it's true, as we're speaking on the phone, though in reality I haven't thought much about her since she left, except when she emails (I always answer promptly). We're not Cynthia and Andy, but in four years, if they're still together, they won't be, either. But what we are seems pretty solid.

Almost asleep, I speculate about what Karp might make of my meeting with Gene Brazil. Perhaps Brazil as the God of Genesis—"Hughie, where wert thou?"—ceremoniously ushering me out of the Garden near the Fluvarium for having stumbled across the forbidden knowledge in the woods. ("But it was an accident! I didn't mean it!") My psyche naked to his all-seeing gaze. Clothe yourself with the skins of righteous industry. Get a life.

But haven't I had one?

NINE

"I've attempted to soften it somewhat in this version," Foley is saying. "I can see that the last one was somewhat too, er, hard-edged, for the readers of the anthology. Something less doctrinaire is warranted. The Timothy McVeigh thing is gone, for starters. I did ponder the possibility of including a pun on 'alienated labour,' but, you'll be glad to know, I thought that would be a bit over the top. But it's hard. You want to be true to yourself, right? I mean it happens to be the case that from the instant your child is born, everything in the world has 'Disney' written on it. It's like the world is telling you who the kid really belongs to."

"True enough."

It's the following day. We're sitting at the kitchen table. Mid-morning, mugs brimming with instant, Foley in full defensive rhetorical mode.

"But what I've tried to do here, I've tried to focus on the illusion that somehow the birth of one's own child is unique, life-affirming, joy-generating, that sort of thing. Do you think that will help?"

"I think getting the word 'joy' in there would be good. Think of the audience for this piece, Foley. They don't want Marxist cowflop. They want to feel good about the idea that men can celebrate the birth of their children."

Foley lets pass the reference to cowflop (a word I don't think I've ever used before), though his momentary silence suggests a rolling of the eyes. We've agreed to disagree, like friends of different faiths. He's often said as much, non-judgmentally identifying me as "liberal."

"Joy, yes, I did put in a 'joy' or two."

"Good. And keep it anecdotal. Like Ryan peeing on the nurse, first thing. But don't allegorize. It wasn't his 'first gesture of defiance of established order,' as per the first draft. He just needed to pee. Your readers will think it's cute."

"Cute," he says, in a so-it's-finally-come-to-this sort of voice.

"Five hundred bucks," I remind him, crass beneficiary of late capitalism that I am.

"I'll put in the thing about peeing on the nurse. And any other comments would be welcome. After you've read it."

"Okay."

"Oh, I almost forgot to tell you. When you were out." There's a note of puzzlement here, and a slight pause. I did disappear for the hour between nine and ten, most uncharacteristic of me, in Foley's experience. He seems a bit hurt that I'm not taking this opportunity to explain. Then he gives me a slip of paper. "Nairn, the fellow said his name was. Ring any bells?"

Rex Nairn, friend of my youth, sort of. The phone number is local. It's been what, fifteen years? More?

Foley has registered my reaction. "Said he was at a B and B downtown. Sounded very friendly."

"Thanks."

He starts to say something, then stops himself.

"What?"

"Well, er, what's with the beard? The absence of the beard. Not, of course, that it's any of my business, but."

"A new start, Foley. No longer concealing myself from the world behind a mask of fur. No more Phantom of the Opera. Don't roll your eyes. As empty symbolic gestures go, this one is (a) cheap, and (b) pretty much risk-free."

Foley pauses, perhaps struggling to come up with something. Finally: "I suspect Maureen will appreciate it."

This hadn't occurred. But he's probably right.

Rex Nairn. Mentioned earlier as the archetypal high-school golden boy *in illo tempore* when he and Cliff MacIntyre and I set out to be men of letters, though his path diverged from ours, Cliff's and mine. No telling how decisions are made in that old yellow wood. While Cliff and I collected degrees, moving through the sheltered mazes of academe, Rex defined himself as the outsider, dropping out of university after a year, travelling Europe, then getting a job at a Toronto publishing house, then becoming a journalist writing mostly about the arts, then an arts bureaucrat in Ottawa, then a freelance writer. He's written profiles of prominent people for magazines and published several books (a popular biography of a Canadian historical figure, a collection of not terribly provocative essays on general cultural topics, a little-read novel in which I think I appear as a buffoon-like minor character, a couple of travel books on off-the-beaten-track Mediterranean islands and remote corners of the British Isles). If that catalogue sounds dismissive, it reflects my disappointment that Rex's golden-boy promise never blossomed into a career commensurate with what everyone (and especially, I think, he) thought was possible, if not inevitable. His life, on balance, seems not much more impressive than mine. But I was never a golden boy.

And none of this really matters. What does matter is that I loved Rex. What a bizarre thing to say. The love of one heterosexual male for another, remaining fairly consistent from boyhood into early manhood. Which explains my need to have distanced myself from him. For this love, my love, has from early on been understandably unrequited. Golden boys don't need friends; they need subordinates, sounding boards, people they can use to affirm their own superiority.

Hence the would-be sort-of friend's need to mock, usually suppressed.

Sandra, meeting Rex once in Ottawa around 1980, proclaimed her instant loathing. "Full of himself," was her banal verdict. I wanted to argue: full of himself, yes, of course, but full to overflowing, so much of himself that it spills over the edges of what is seemly. Sandra was not interested in pursuing the subject.

I think it was on that occasion, or perhaps on another visit a year or two later, Rex still in his arts bureaucrat period, that we were having lunch at a restaurant in the Market when he bellowed, apropos of not much: "I'm in love." He beamed pointedly. Two women at the next table, startled, glanced at us, then looked away. "In love," he continued. "A woman named Betsy. She's in Toronto. Thank God for the government phone system. We can talk every day." He paused to sip his Perrier. I looked again at the next table, the women there pretending to be absorbed in their own conversation. They were younger than we were, chic. It occurred to me that Rex was enjoying the audience. Or maybe he really was oblivious.

"Words of love flowing through the miles between here and Toronto. Taxpayers' money spent in the service of love!" He paused again, making sure I understood that he'd performed magic of the highest order, dross turned to gold, benighted citizens unwittingly contributing to his happiness. His, Rex's.

"I haven't told Helen yet. But it's a matter of time. Betsy comes here on weekends. Helen suspects nothing. It's sad, sad. For her. But I have no choice. This thing with Betsy, it's powerful. Love must have its way."

This drew a snicker from the next table, but Rex decided not to notice. I risk a quick peek. One of the women appeared entranced by Rex's performance, lips slightly parted, gaze fixed. Rex, I had to remind myself, was an attractive man, yet another instance of life's unfairness. The other woman, though, the source of the snicker, clearly annoyed by her friend's attitude of reverence, was occupied in getting her things together.

"One waits a lifetime for something like this." It is of course understood that I myself might wait several lifetimes for something like this, but that's not the point: he wants to convey a sense of his good fortune, to share it with me, as one who has always taken an interest in his good fortune. "There have been other important women, but nothing like this." "Important"—that choice of adjective is pure Rex. One can imagine its appearance in some scrupulously researched academic study: "Of the myriad women who figure in the sexual history of Rex Nairn, some of the more important are…" And he's so earnest, so unaware of his own self-absorption. Of course I feel a kind of contempt for him at such moments, but admiration, too, at the way he can be carried away by his own performance.

"Helen will come to understand what's at issue. She must."

This was my cue, or would have been, in the old days. My line: something witty and crude, so that we could acknowledge the inflated rhetoric without really challenging it, something we could pretend would take us back before Betsy, before Helen, before the existence of females.

Only this time I couldn't do it. Instead I let him wind down without interruption, nodding with false empathy.

That was about a quarter-century ago. We correspond occasionally, via email, brief exchanges once or twice a year. And before that, short letters, the odd phone call. After a time it became evident that Betsy was not going to be mentioned again. Helen, I came to assume, understood all too well what was at issue and had found a way to make Rex understand it too. But that's my speculation only, Rex's confidences not extending to anything that might make him look less than completely in control.

That's my Rex.

Back in the present, Foley is poring over a pamphlet I've left on the kitchen counter, souvenir of my morning's outing. "'Benign Prostatic Hyperplasia?'"

"That's what it says, yes." I'm in no mood for a cheery discussion of this document. My mysterious lost hour of the morning has been spent in a visit, to a (now "my") urologist, Dr. Matthew O'Dell. "It's very large," he told me. "Right at the end of the Bell curve. Sooner or later we'll have to do a TURP. For now we can get by with tamsulosin. Pills, which you'll have to take every night at bedtime. But a prostate that size, sooner or later you'll have difficulty voiding. Once you're in retention, you'll have no choice. Catheter, then, when we can schedule it—and I have to tell you, O.R. time is at a premium—the TURP. You might want to get on the list for that now."

He paused, waiting for me to ask what a TURP is. His posture and expression conveyed a kind of intensity, a puppydog seriousness that reminded me of Eddie Laskowski, our department's now departed post-everythingist, explaining why the issue of how we know that we know something so engrosses him, and how he can work it into his article on DeLillo. And (implicit) how he doesn't give a flying fuck for what you think, as long as you can say something to confirm his sense of intellectual superiority.

This was probably unfair to Dr. O'Dell, peering at me through his horn-rimmed glasses with the careful non-expression of a man twenty years one's junior who knows something important about oneself that one doesn't. To him I was a piece of meat. Sentient, yes, but that was a fact of minor significance. He would not treat me with obvious contempt, but neither would he honour me with any gesture of informality.

I decided not to ask him what a TURP is. At that point I didn't even know it was an acronym. Instead I said, "I don't think I want to get on that list just yet."

Dr. O'Dell almost sighed. "Your call. But I suggest you think it over."

The eyes, brown, bore into me, self-righteous. Who was I to question the immutable laws of nature? My prostate is huge and getting huger. Resistance is futile.

Outstared, I looked around the windowless office. Nothing on the walls. No family photos (though he was wearing a ring), no poster about urinary-tract disorders, nothing. An ascetic, devoted to his discipline, possessor of classified secrets of genitalia. Images strictly forbidden.

He could've learned a thing or two from Dr. Sherry Kirsch.

"Read these," he said, shoving a couple of pamphlets at me. He wrote the prescription while I glanced at the first question of the BPH Quiz: "The function of the prostate is to (a) produce sperm; (b) store urine; (c) produce fluid in which sperm travel." Until today I've had no reason to be interested in such matters. I was pretty sure (b) is wrong, though.

When I looked up, O'Dell smiled, his one attempt to be human: it was the ironic, teeth-revealing, over-deliberate smile of someone who knows its target will have reason not to reciprocate. "Get this filled today. I'll see you in six months. Barb in the outer office will set it up. Unless something comes up before then. Clear?" I was dismissed.

Back in the car, I flipped through the larger and glossier of the two pamphlets, until I came to a drawing of a doctor (actually the disembodied head of a doctor, surgically capped and masked, and the disembodied hand of a doctor, surgically gloved). The doctor was staring through a microscope-type viewing thingy at one end of what looked like a very long syringe. The syringe extended through a grade-school-crude outline of a penis (so identified in capital letters, lest the reader be uncertain). At the far end of the penis, the syringe poked into a shaded bulb-like object labelled "prostate" (also capitalized). Underneath was the caption: "Transurethral resection of the prostate (TURP)."

Such is the fate to which my body has betrayed me. But I'll stay off the list for as long as I can. I drove home in a bit of a daze.

"So," Foley says. He's found the page with the diagram. "Looks like medieval torture. Or maybe something the CIA would come up with."

"Thank you for that insight. But it's not going to happen anytime soon."

"Hey, it says that after you've had this thing done, you can't father a child, but, and I'm quoting, 'it does not interfere with the ability to have and enjoy normal sexual activity.' Just like a vasectomy. Kewl."

"Silver lining, Foley."

I feel irrationally reluctant to phone Rex. A desire to delay gratification? A concern that I'll be disappointing him in some way? Or that he'll disappoint me? All of the above, possibly.

When the phone rings, I'm relieved that it's not him. And surprised that it's Andy, calling from work. He's never done this before.

"So, what did you think of Cynthia?" Who else would start a conversation by asking a question like that of some-one who is, at best, a casual acquaintance?

"I thought she was...very nice, Andy. I liked her."

"Did you really? I'm so pleased to hear that. Really." He says this with such intensity that I believe him. But I have no idea what, if anything, I'm now supposed to say.

"I know it probably seems a bit weird," Andy goes on, "but I'm always a little apprehensive about how people are going to respond to her. As I mentioned earlier." He pauses. "I mean, you know, the enthusiasm about her thesis. And related subject matter. Sometimes people think it's a bit much. As in, why doesn't she shut up about it? Do you know what I mean?"

"Well, I have to say that wasn't my reaction. I think it's good when people are enthusiastic about what they do."

"You're lying, Hugh. I can tell. But you're a good sport. I appreciate it."

How should I answer this? I'm not actually lying, though it's true that candour is something I'm not as familiar with as I like to think I used to be. And on reflection, I suppose I am lying, sort of.

"Andy, I—"

"You don't really know what to say to that, do you? That's okay. People usually don't. But I've found that it's best to get things out in the open."

I have the disquieting feeling that Andy is gathering strength, gearing up to perform some feat of verbal acrobatics that will leave me gasping for hypocritical breath.

"I mean," he continues, "if friends can't trust each other to be truthful, what's the point? Yes, the truth can be uncomfortable. If you'd said something negative about Cynthia, I might find it hurtful. But that's a risk you need to take."

"It's true," I say, "that she wasn't quite what I was expecting. But I'm not sure now what that would have been. Some hypothetical female counterpart to you, I suppose. Whatever that would be." I have the distinct sense that I'm digging myself in deeper, so I say, "I have the distinct sense that I'm digging myself in deeper."

Andy laughs, a shade too triumphantly. "Aha. You see. Now you *are* starting to tell the truth. And it's no problem for me. Now, 'fess up. The real truth is that you thought she was—what is that local expression?—*a pain in the hole.* Isn't that right?"

Time to make a stand. "No. No, it isn't right. Yes, it's true that she got a bit carried away when she was talking about her thesis. But I thought that was endearing. And I thought it was nice, the way you kept encouraging her. Very supportive. You cared more about that than whether I was into it or not. I think you do love her deeply." (Why am I talking like this? This doesn't sound like me.) "And I'm sure that she's worthy of your love." (Yes, I actually have said "worthy of your love.")

"Okay," Andy says. "She's 'worthy of my love.' I'll take it. And one more thing, and I'm telling you this with Cynthia's permission but please don't mention it when you see her again but I think it's important for people who care about us to know: she thinks she may be an abductee herself. I've got to go now, there's a meeting I have to be at."

Dialogue with Andy, I reflect, always seems somehow unreal, as though it takes place in some alternate realm of consciousness, set apart from ordinary experience. Which would certainly also describe any conversation I'd be likely to have with Rex Nairn, and for which I still don't feel quite ready. I decide to escape to the university for an hour or two.

It's exam time for the oddly named "Spring" semester, which in fact runs from early May to mid-August, so there aren't many students to be seen—a few sitting on benches catching some rays as they pore over their notes, clusters of three or four smoking near building entrances, and inside, the occasional classroom full of young men and women bent over their booklets, pens moving arhythmically, like tiny oars manipulated by out-of-sync galley slaves.

I check my mailbox, not that I'm expecting anything important. Snail-mail is the bailiwick of the irrelevant and the redundant. So I'm surprised to find a large internal-mail envelope with my name on it in handwriting familiar for its ornate elegance.

Bernadette O'Keefe, of course. I open it in my office. It's a photocopy of a journal article, authored by one Lister B. Craddock. "This is what we're up against," Bernadette has written in the top margin.

The article is titled "'P.S. I Love You': The Postscript as Transgressive Apocalypse." Casting my eye down the page, I see sentences such as "This little-studied literary device deserves sophisticated academic scrutiny…The postscript by its very positioning suggests a powerful analogy with the Christian Book of Revelation…This omega of epistolary discourse, always seen as mere appendage to that which has preceded it, must now be understood in terms of its ability to resist and subvert the thrust of the main text of the letter.…" And so on.

The "exemplary post-scriptor," it soon develops, is T. S. Eliot (the subject of Lister's dissertation). The main thrust of the article is that, through tortured analysis, any seemingly innocuous Eliotic postscript can be construed to

143

"significantly modify, undercut, overturn, or generally dis-
arrange" any common-sense interpretation of the letter to
which it is appended. A prime example: "When you have
copies ready for signing, let me know where the signature
ought to be put. I have numbered the copies you gave me."
Not as simple and banal as you might think, Lister asserts.
"The irony of the evidently straight-faced request for information about the placement of the signature," he writes,
"is, of course, that the expression of this request is located
directly below the signature itself. The obvious allusions to
Plato and Boehme reinforce the sense that this postscript is
a meditation on the nature of authenticity and originality.
Eliot, despite his apparent submissiveness (the request for
direction from the letter's addressee), has nonetheless con-
comitantly declared his own godlike potency, having *himself*
numbered the copies, as the biblical deity is said to have
numbered the hairs on the head of the psalmist. How this
is related to the outwardly mundane content of the body of
the letter is worthy of detailed investigation…"—an investigation that occupies another three pages, which I decide
not to peruse.

I've never been a fan of Lister, but I feel a certain sadness on his behalf. Imagine having to pretend to believe in
the importance of this crap, or (worse) actually to believe
in it. He's an angry-seeming young guy, Lister, much given
to making caustic pronouncements and asking belligerently
phrased questions in department meetings. He radiates a
general sense of entitlement that many colleagues find less
than endearing. In corridor conversation, he lets it slip that
perhaps another university might be better able to accommodate his career aspirations, and that one of these years

we may just have to learn to do without him. That this is not a particularly daunting prospect for most of us seems not to have registered.

But here, in the article, is the other side of Lister—the poor, bare, forked scholar that we all were once, struggling to make his name in the pages of *The Journal of Literary Irrelevance* (or whatever it is), all the big fish having by now long since been fried, trying to survive on a diet of leftover minnows. His ironic T-shirts and finally fashionable ultra-short hair ("Good morning, Mr. Zip Zip Zip,") won't help him here.

Of course Bernadette is right. I'm sure she understands that what we're "up against" is not Lister himself but the *Zeitgeist* that has produced him. And there ain't much we can do about that. It does seem a bit extreme of her to have tracked down the article, though, and I wonder for a moment if she harbours some delusion of inflicting professional harm on Lister through public exposure of the idiocy of his research. Good luck with that. But no, she'll have known better; the article is for my eyes only, a joke that only dinosaurs like ourselves can appreciate.

Bill Duffett is in his office, a fact which reminds me that his interview with the headship search committee was scheduled for earlier today.

"It was awful," he says with some glee. "They tore me to shreds. Plush quoted from your letter. I won't have a chance now. Thank God."

There's a take-it-or-leave-it blandness to Duffett's face. You'd never infer the relentlessly ironic take on the world associated with its possessor. Bill is one of the few Newfoundlanders left in the department, a holdover from the era when the university was essentially a glorified high school. He's gliding serenely toward retirement, as many of us are, the drab colours of his sweaters and pants seemingly designed to help him blend in to the bleak institutional backdrop that is our workplace.

"Plush quoted from my letter?"

"The part where you said something about 'a department teeming with eccentric and difficult colleagues,' or something like that. Wanted to know if I shared that view. If this is characteristic of the mindset of my supporters, what are the chances of my promoting collegial harmony, she wanted to know. And then she batted at me."

Rita Plush is Alice Plover's major ally. Bill is referring to her habit of batting her eyes in a mock-coquettish way to suggest that her apparently naïve question has certainly blown you out of the water, hasn't it? It has apparently not occurred to her that it's somewhat ridiculous for a woman of any age, let alone sixty, to be batting her eyes, no matter how sarcastically she's doing it.

"And what did you say?"

"That I respected your opinion, of course." He's beaming.

"You really really don't want this job, do you?"

"Norman, I agreed to let my name stand. I've done my duty."

"That you don't want the job is, as I said in the letter, the best possible reason that you should have it."

"I know, Norman, I know." He shakes his head, parodying sadness. "Then Power asked what I'd do to make sure that we all taught the same number of students."

"But that's impossible." Impossible because troglodytes like Barney Power are unfit or afraid to teach low-enrolment graduate or senior undergraduate courses.

"When I pointed that out, Power said, 'So you have no plan to equalize workload.' He looked very smug."

"Well, congratulations, I guess. You're off the hook. Welcome to the Alice Plover era."

"We need to celebrate. Beer. Friday at four?"

"Agreed."

I've completely forgotten to mention that I found a dead body yesterday.

"And Norman?"

"Yes?"

"What unfortunate accident has befallen your face?"

Driving home, I allow thoughts of Cliff MacIntyre to arise (or is it descend?). He would have found the campus I've just left a much more congenial workplace than I do. He would have ignored the fact that many of his colleagues were dim-witted or unpleasant. He would have kept his head down and become even more productive, establishing himself as something of a loner but respected by everyone for his stubborn fair-mindedness. He might even have made friends with Bill Duffett, though his abstemiousness would have precluded Friday afternoon conversations over beer. But they could have gone running together. He would not have been interested in gossip, would not have been irritated by lazy or dishonest students, would not have suffered from a vague sense of unfulfilment. He would not have committed adultery, would not have been divorced. He would, conceivably, have been happy.

I pass the cemetery on the way up Mayor Avenue. Sometimes St. John's manifests itself as one vast multi-faceted *memento mori*, carefully positioned so that some fresh version of death will always be staring back at me.

Survivor's guilt. Who knew?

———

Rex Nairn, or at least a somewhat bloated and bewrinkled simulacrum of him, is beaming and extending a hand. "Hey sport, how are you making it," he says.

It's a line from a Robert Creeley poem. Somehow it's become our traditional salutation, written or oral. Black Mountain poetry was his discovery, superseding Irving Layton, and he was welcome to it, as far as I was concerned, characterized, as it seemed to me, by pretentious and unrewarding obscurity. But Creeley's humour was accessible to both of us, and so that line became a permanent part of our dialogue.

"Hey," I say, extending my own hand. "Who let you in?" We're standing in my living room, Foley hovering in the background.

"Young Terry here was kind enough to invite me in for a cup of tea. When I dropped by unannounced. It's good to see you."

He sounds like he means it. I reply in kind.

He's looking pretty good, Rex is, despite the years. His posture seems designed to suggest the idea of "dignity." If I have to move, his body and facial expression seem to declare, I will do so with due deliberation. I will not be hurried or moved along. I'm the guy most worth paying attention to in this room. I have a neatly trimmed silvery beard. I have an expensive haircut. I'm aging gracefully. I still have sufficient resources of charm and good looks to be getting on with. Not bad, hey?

"I was about to leave," Foley volunteers, clearly not pleased at being referred to as "young Terry." He is, after all, something like thirty-four.

"I understand Terry is a budding journalist," Rex says, rather more loudly than necessary. "I was telling him about my career. Freelancing is not for the faint of heart."

Has he implicitly placed me in that category, someone for whom security has been everything? Probably not. It's all about him. I note that Foley winces at the word "budding." He's been at it for about four years now, in a jack-of-all-tradesy way, managing—more or less—to survive economically, something I wouldn't have dreamed him capable of.

"I must be off," Foley says quickly. "Nice meeting you, Mr. Nairn." He delivers that line with a tad more deference than I'm comfortable with. Obviously the fabled Nairn charm can still do its thing. And part of me wants Foley to be impressed with my cool old friend. Still, he's not that impressive, is he?

Rex does a quick scan of the art on the walls, not commenting. The artists are all local. There's no way he would have heard of any of them.

"So," he says finally, turning back to me. "No Blackwoods?"

He nods, satisfied. The fact that he has established that he knows who Blackwood is is probably meant to signal he's up to speed on Newfoundland culture. "What am I doing here, you're probably wondering."

This doesn't require a response.

"Well, officially, I'm researching a travel piece. For an international high-end publication you probably haven't heard of. And what I write can't be conventional touristy stuff. I want to get into the psyche of the place, give a sense of what makes it tick, focusing on the arts."

"Cool."

"So I'm here for five days. I've got a bunch of interviews lined up. There's a lot happening here, hey?"

"Yep."

"My editors think St. John's could become a cultural destination. You're smiling, but this place is becoming hot stuff. As you well know. Some of your ex-students have been making names for themselves, haven't they?"

This is true, though it's got little to do with me. I nod in such a way as to simulate an appropriate degree of modest assent.

"It's a creative ferment, the editors think. Convey some sense of the excitement of being inside a ferment, they told me. So that's what I'm here for. Ferment."

We both chuckle at this one, the old adolescent take on the world, perhaps our strongest bond, briefly flickering into life.

"But you said 'officially.'"

"Yes, well, unofficially." He pauses, and I know what's coming. "Unofficially, I'm going to be joined by someone. Much easier to be together away from one's usual context. You understand."

He knows I do. I decide to postpone the ritual question about Helen and the kids.

"She'll be flying in the day after tomorrow, actually. Remarkable woman. You must meet her."

"It would be an honour."

"Well. In the meantime, why don't you let me buy you lunch? On my expense account. Then you can drive me around for a bit." A pause. "Unless, of course, you have more important things to do." The tone indicates that he regards this as an unlikely prospect.

"I'm at your service."

As we leave the house, he says, "Terry tells me that your, er, partner is unfortunately not on the scene this week. I would've liked to meet her." And then: the quick glance down at my deformed hand, as though to verify that, despite everything, I'm the same *lusus naturae* I've always been. And how the hell have I managed to attract a partner?

"Yes," I tell him, "it is unfortunate."

TEN

It's midafternoon, and I'm giving Rex the grand tour, though what exactly that will consist of after we've done Signal Hill, I'm not sure. We've had lunch downtown and covered all the conventional bases. There has been a brief discussion of Maureen; Rex has said he "looks forward" to reading her book. Other topics have included family—I've filled him in on Emily and Sandra; he's spoken affectionately of Helen—"She's put up with a lot, over the years," he's said, rather complacently—and his two sons, one a dentist now, the other a lawyer. He's listened politely to my detailed explanation of my interest in the work of Richard Karp; I've listened politely to his plans for a novel, something to do with the Group of Seven. He's winced sympathetically at my description of the TURP; I've made sympathetic noises as he's described his struggle with tinnitus.

Then we moved on to his impressions of St. John's. Is it the case, he's wondered, that there's a certain facial type or types that could fairly be described as characteristic of Newfoundlanders, and if so, would Foley be a good example? I've suggested that he should entertain the possibility that St. John's is somewhat more cosmopolitan than he may have imagined. And I've tried to fill him in on important events in Newfoundland history little known on the mainland—the sealing disaster of 1914, Beaumont Hamel, the loss of responsible government in the thirties, the Confederation debate, resettlement. (He has heard about Churchill Falls and the Ocean Ranger, though.)

At one point he's said, "You really like it here, don't you?" Evidently he's always thought of me as being in some kind of exile, banished by my inability to function in the real world of, well, Ontario.

I've persuaded him to leave his rental car at my house, so that I can play the role of guide—not a native informant, exactly, but the next thing to it. "That wasn't bad at all," he's said, of the meal, as though surprised that Duckworth Street could meet his sophisticated culinary expectations. "Show me the town."

On the way up Signal Hill, just after I've drawn his attention to Dead Man's Pond on our left, he brings up the subject of Cliff, for the first time.

"So Cliff is no longer with us."

"Nope."

"And then there were two. And here we are together again. Some coincidence, hey?"

I haven't realized that he's still been thinking of us as a triumvirate. And I'm not sure what to reply. Then he asks for details—my original email to him was terse—and I provide him with a summary of Arlene's email to me.

By now we've pulled into the parking lot at the top. There's the usual summer gaggle of tourists photographing each other with the calm blue-grey infinity as the backdrop, checking out Cabot Tower, the more adventurous going down (or, very slowly, back up) the long flight of steps leading to the hiking trail closer to the water.

I recall that his father died suddenly, heart attack, at sixty-three. One year to go, he may be thinking. It happened at a traffic light, his father alone in the car, no warning signs.

"So it was preventable" is his last comment before we get out. "That's sad."

An odd moral to draw, but consistent with his way of dealing with the world. If it was preventable, he, in similar circumstances, would have found a way to prevent it. He would not have succumbed, as Cliff had. So now he has nothing to fear—except, of course the fear that impels him to find that reassuring meaning and no other in the Cliff-death story.

"So this is where Marconi did his thing," he says, reading a plaque by the low stone wall at the sea-facing edge of the parking lot.

"Yep. Just over there, actually." I point to the small hill at the far end of the lot, thinking God this is boring. "Used to be a hospital there."

We make our way around the other side of the Tower, to get the best view of the Narrows, the harbour, and the city itself. I remember the day I first touched down in Newfoundland, twenty-two years ago. Dr. Fabian O'Callahan, the department head, met me at the airport and whisked me up here first thing, not bothering to stop at my hotel. It was late April, cold and grey, snow still on the ground. He didn't talk about Marconi or the historical strategic value of the harbour, just marched me around the parking lot asking what I thought of it all. I can't remember what I told him. He seemed anxious to get it over with, as though it were some necessary but dull ritual. So now I'm in his position? Bizarre.

"During the war they had nets strung across the Narrows so German submarines couldn't get in," I tell Rex. He nods, looking abstracted. I point out the Basilica, the Rooms beside it, the Confederation Building, the university.

"Would you say this is the psychological epicentre of the place?"

"What?"

"I think you heard me. On one side, the vast ocean, emblem of what? The collective unconscious, let's say. On the other, the human community, the ego. The Narrows, the point at which one flows into the other. Or meets the other, I guess it doesn't exactly flow."

I'm not sure whether he's being ironic. The tone suggests not.

"And here, where we can look down on this process, bring it to full consciousness, articulate it—*this* is the sacred space, the *temenos*."

"*Temenos*, is it?"

"Sacred space. Greek. How would that be for an opening paragraph? I could present it as the insight that unlocks the mystery of the creativity of the place. Marconi as the figure of the artist works, too. Receiving the signals from the other side of the cosmos, then interpreting them for the locals."

"Well, it's not really an *insight*, is it? Would your editors go for something like that?"

"They'd lap it up."

"And then of course you'd have to say something convincing about the mystery you've unlocked."

"Yes, well, I've got five days to figure that out." He's writing something in a notebook. "Listen, how does this sound: 'It's not for nothing that locals will, as if driven by some unconscious force, insist that newcomers begin their exploration of St. John's with a visit to Signal Hill?'"

"You were actually driven in my unconscious Corolla."

"Just doing my job. And I didn't mean to imply that *you're* a local. Don't take it personally."

(And I can't help thinking about what Richard Karp would make of this place. Let's see: an elevated location overlooking a city, excellent spot for the temptation of a Christ-figure. "All these things will I give thee, if thou wilt fall down and worship me." The Karp protagonist would turn away from the barely audible proposition, uttered no doubt in the shadow of the Tower by the false friend whose aim was the ruin of his listener. Or not. Karp did not shy away from examining the nature of evil. Perhaps his character would have acquiesced to the suggestion, would have jumped at the chance to enjoy the kingdoms of the world and their glory. Perhaps, it occurs to me, Rex himself would have done that.)

As we head down the hill, I tell him about my discovery of the corpse.

"Wow," he says, but in a neutral tone, to imply that there's nothing really extraordinary here, nothing that would have fazed him. "So you're a person of interest."

"More like a person of irrelevance, I'd say."

"But given the way the justice system works here, aren't you a bit concerned?"

"Not really. I'm innocent, after all."

"But what if they can't find whoever did it? They could try to pin it on you."

"Good luck to them."

He seems mildly put out that I'm not worried. I doubt he has any sinister agenda here. It's just that he likes to think things are more dramatic than they are. Then he decides to drop it.

"Where are we going?"

"I thought a spin around Quidi Vidi." In truth, I'm finding it difficult to come up with an itinerary that will take us more than twenty minutes. What else is there for a visitor to see in this town? More specifically, what would Rex be interested in seeing? (Here's the harbour, the repository of our raw sewage. Note the picturesque Irving Oil tanks gracing the Southside Hills. Here on Cochrane Street is the plaque denoting the former residence of Johnny Burke, of whom you've never heard. Here, just past the courthouse on Duckworth, is the aptly named Church Hill, which will take us past the major Anglican, United, and Presbyterian churches; if it's after dark, note the presence of the strung-out hookers on the street corners.)

As is the case with any city, everything important is invisible.

"Not bad," he says, when I try that out on him. "Bullshit, of course, but it sounds good. You haven't lost your touch."

And of course I'm both pleased at this and ashamed to be.

At the bottom of the hill I've taken a hard right on the street that goes past Belbin's Grocery. "A legend," I tell Rex, who makes vague polite noises in response. I don't feel like explaining how an ordinary-looking pint-size grocery store could become "a legend." I'm beginning to find my tour-guide persona irritating. From now on, if Rex wants to know stuff, he can ask.

Another right at Forest Road.

"What was that institutional-looking building where we turned?"

"Her Majesty's Penitentiary."

The conversation shifts to Rex's slate of upcoming interviews. He wants my take on a number of members of the local arts community, many of whom I know. But not all, and there are even some writers I've never met. He asks about a couple of my former students who've become nationally recognized novelists. But they don't live here anymore. He mentions some film people, including Raissa. This time I don't acknowledge the connection. I feel strangely protective of her, though what does she have to fear from Rex? Misrepresentation, no doubt, but that wouldn't be affected by anything I said to him. Then I realize that it's possessiveness. She's mine. If he knew she was mine, he'd somehow try to take her away. How would he do that? And what would that even mean?

Grow the fuck up.

We've slowed down for the narrow streets of Quidi Vidi Village, emerged onto the misleadingly named Boulevard at the east end of the pond, driven past the military base at Pleasantville—not much of a sightseeing excursion, an ordinary small body of water on our left, not by any stretch "scenic," but it's there. People walk and run around it. It's the site of the annual Regatta ("oldest sporting event in North America," or is it "oldest continuously held sporting event in North America"?).

"It would seem," Rex says, "that First Nations people didn't have sporting events." The ironic edge is still there, aimed both at the cluelessness of Eurocentrism and at the prissiness of politically correct discourse. I can hear the scare quotes around "First Nations." It's like we're still maybe sixteen.

"Where to now? Is there anything in particular you'd like to see?"

"Well, I'd like to check out The Rooms, of course, but I want to save that" (so he can take his girlfriend, obviously). "But what do you suggest? What about your own personal St. John's?"

"Don't really have one. You've been to the house. The university's not worth seeing, except maybe for the president's new quarter-million dollar private washroom, but that's probably off-limits for tourists. We could drive up and down Duckworth and Water Street a few times. We could head out to Cape Spear, 'easternmost point of land in North America.'"

He hears my own scare quotes and snorts affably. "I think I might save that one, too. And it's kind of out of the way, isn't it?"

"A half-hour drive, maybe."

There's a pause. I'm thinking he's decided that another hour in my company would be somewhat more than he'd like to bargain for. Then he says, "Okay, I've got it. Take me to the scene of the crime. Where you found the body."

"Why? What a wacky idea. There's nothing to see."

"Humour me. Since we've got nothing better to do."

On the way, I tell him that I find the whole idea a little unnerving. "What if the cops are still there doing forensic stuff or something, and they ask us for ID and they tell that detective? It'd look bad, wouldn't it?"

"But you're innocent and you have faith in the justice system."

"It doesn't make sense to complicate things unnecessarily."

"What I'm thinking," he says, "is this. Cliff dies. You inform me of that fact. A short time after that, you stumble across a body when you're out for a walk. Then I show up out of the blue. There's no causation here. These things happened independently of each other. I'd planned this trip long before Cliff died, if that's what you're thinking. No causation, but there's a pattern."

"You're not going to bring predestination into this, are you?" Rex is a lapsed Presbyterian. When we were kids and he screwed up in some minor way, he'd sometimes invoke predestination as the reason, thereby exculpating himself, he believed. And now he doesn't seem to find my question funny.

"Not predestination exactly. Have you read much Jung?"

"Not Jung himself, only some of the *Coles Notes*-level interpretations. The minimum required to teach *Fifth Business*, let's say."

"Well. I've become quite interested in some of his writings. In fact I joined a Jung study group a couple of years ago. It's been very...useful."

"I see." Maybe this is a sign of early senility? No, that's an unkind thought. Still, who would've thunk it? It's difficult to picture Rex as the respectful student of anything other than himself.

And maybe I've been selling him short for decades. Who knows?

We've been driving up New Cove Road, and I turn left at Elizabeth, heading west. Last time I did this, I was coming home from my visit to Dr. Sherry Kirsch.

"So there's a certain synchronicity at work here," Rex is saying. "I think it would be psychically healthy for us to visit the place where you encountered death. As we remember Cliff."

"Healthy how?"

"To confront, vicariously, the reality of death. Look it in the eye. So to speak."

I'm trying hard to find irony in the tone, but I'm not sure it's there, except for the last phrase. I try to inject some myself.

"Isn't the idea of 'vicarious confrontation' sort of an oxymoron?"

But he's not biting. "Not really. I mean Death isn't going to show up wearing a black hood and carrying a sickle, is he? But at least we can say, We know you're there. It doesn't bother us. We're Alive." I can hear the capital A, loud and clear.

"We'll be there in less than ten."

"Good. Good."

Looking to fill up the conversational space, I ask Rex if he's kept in touch with anyone else from high school. One or two, he says, and that keeps us going until we pull into the Fluvarium parking lot. No police cars, at least.

"So," Rex says. "Lead me into the valley of death."

"Right this way."

We head down the bricked walkway that goes past the main entrance to the Fluvarium, cross the wooden footbridge over Leary's Brook, the water low and sluggish at this time of year, then turn right onto the side path that leads to the woods.

We're not speaking now, as though our bogus mission requires a code of silence. Less than five minutes from the parking lot and we're there. Yellow police tape demarcates the area, but there's no one around. Rex ducks under the tape. I hesitate.

"Come on," he says. "This won't hurt a bit."

I follow him. There's plenty of room. It's at least the size of a boxing ring, maybe bigger.

"So the body was where?"

"About where you're standing."

There's no sign that anyone was here, though. I could be making it all up, for all he knows.

Rex gradually lowers himself toward the ground. At first I think he's going to kneel, but he settles for a kind of awkward squatting posture. He doesn't say anything. And he doesn't move for what seems a long time, maybe thirty seconds. Eyes closed. Finally he gets up.

"What was that about?"

"I was envisioning my own death," he says. "And, of course, rebirth. I find such gestures to be mildly cathartic."

"I see."

He ducks under the tape and we start back along the path.

"And it should be cathartic for you to have witnessed that," he goes on. "Now you can connect the experience to me. You don't have to see it in terms of some anonymous nobody. The next step is to understand it in terms of yourself."

"What?"

"To see yourself as the victim. And the killer, the one who survives the encounter and moves on."

"Actually"—and this occurs to me only now—"I do know who the killer is." And I tell Rex about Mr. Don't-fuck-with-me, the thug I saw walking around the pond just before I found the body. And I see that he had the tattoo of a teardrop under his left eye, something I wasn't aware of until this moment.

Rex listens patiently, then says "Of course there's a 'real' killer, but that's the least interesting aspect of this whole business."

I can't think of anything to say to that. By now we're out of the woods, literally at least, and I wonder how this would look to a passerby: two geezers emerging from a private conference among the trees. What could we have been up to?

"Death," he says, as we trudge up the walkway toward the parking lot, "always reminds me of Brad Coulter. First person I knew who died. Same for you, if I'm not mistaken."

Brad Coulter was killed in a motorcycle accident the summer after Cliff moved away, just before our last year of high school. Coulter was an anomaly, any way you slice it: anarchy personified, not in the by-then-clichéd James Dean sense, but in some way we had no language for. Though he was disruptive in all the traditional ways—smartass answers, mimicking the teacher's voice, laughing too loudly at the teacher's jokes, and so on—his persona didn't fit that of the stereotypical class clown. At the point when, after he had the class laughing with him, just then he'd somehow contrive to imitate the sound of our laughter, to do it with just the element of exaggeration necessary for satirical edge, to let us know that he was not with *us*, that we were as worthy of ridicule as the teacher.

He could make excellent fart noises when the teacher's back was turned, but was too much the artist ever to fart for real. Outside the classroom, he was a mystery. He had no friends as far as anyone knew, and what he did after school and on weekends was equally unknown. He had a mesomorph's compact athletic body but no interest in sports. He radiated nervous energy even when he was sitting still, which wasn't often. Even his curly black hair suggested arrested motion, waves improbably static for a fraction of a second before their release into violence.

He was alone when the accident happened, of course, not being a member of a gang or club, no other vehicle involved, according to the brief story in the paper. No one at school even knew he *had* a motorcycle. If there was a funeral, nobody we knew went to it.

"Coulter," I say back to Rex. "Yes."

We drive back to my place, trading anecdotes about Ernie Clark, our football coach and Phys Ed teacher. Clark was the teacher we loved, his style rooted in sarcasm, and, we surmised, a deep cynicism underlying it. Constructive criticism was, to him, a language as foreign as Swahili. The reminiscences are convoluted, their humour context-dependent, opaque to outsiders. You had to be there. And for a few minutes we are, we're back there, exchanging our renditions of the distinctive Ernie Clark muted snorting noise, the sound of an attempt to clear the nasal passages without there being anything to clear, something he did at least once per sentence. We relive some of the classic putdowns, the ones that would begin with "We mustn't laugh at Norman" (or Nairn, or whoever) and would then evolve into a concisely phrased inventory of the target's shortcomings. We recall the one-liners. ("We didn't expect you girls to actually *make the tackle*, but couldn't you have tried to grab his sweater as he ran past?") We're going past the damn cemetery between Empire and Newtown before we run out of material.

He declines my offer to come in for a drink. (His rental is parked in front, so he doesn't need to be driven anywhere.) "Must prepare for my interviews tomorrow," he says.

"Who's up first?"

"This Zachary Philip Dwyer guy. I couldn't get through his book. Gave up after twenty pages. Does it get any better?"

"No." Dwyer's novel, *Up to Me Arse in Muck*, has been successfully marketed as the best book so far produced by a "new" generation of Newfoundland writers. It features an airheaded young male protagonist who drinks, tokes, and screws his way to nowhere in particular. It's been well received on the mainland, mostly, I suspect, because it reinforces every stereotype about Newfoundland ever conceived of, a paradigm of the Newfoundlandish equivalent of bojangling.

"Any suggestion as to what I might ask him?"

"Just let him talk, not that you'll have a choice. You'll hear how he's on the side of the dispossessed, the outcast, the drug addict, the alcoholic, the homeless, those despised by bourgeois society. It'll be pretty much cut and paste from that tradition. You might hear about Charles Bukowski and his ilk as inspirations. Maybe Hubert Selby Junior, but Dwyer's knowledge of literary history probably doesn't go back that far. Oh, and you'll hear about how Canada has exploited Newfoundland, that sort of thing. Local boilerplate."

"Good, good. Just what I needed to know. I'll be in touch."

"See you anon. Sport."

ELEVEN

The house is empty. (Foley's comings and goings are erratic, unpredictable.) There are four phone messages, the first from Raissa McCloskey: "Dah-ling," she begins (her signature ironic phone salutation), "you know Aaron's doing his show this week, right?" (I have seen it advertised somewhere, possibly heard it mentioned on the radio.) "Anyway, I've been in touch with him, and he's getting me comps for tomorrow. Here's the thing. I'd like you to come, if you're not doing anything more exciting—that's a joke, by the way—and come with me to have a beer with him after. I want to pitch my movie idea to him, and I'd like you to help me. Since you were so supportive when I told you about it. You were supportive, weren't you? That's how I remember it, anyway. So let me know, okay?"

The second message is from Gene Brazil: "Dr. Norman? I'd like to have another chat with you. A few things have come up. I think you can help me out. Call as soon as you can." He gives the number twice, slowly. The tone is neutral, institutional, and of course I feel panic. What things could have "come up" that I could conceivably "help" him "out" with? I decide not to call back immediately.

The third message is from Bernadette O'Keefe: "Hugh, I'd like to discuss something with you. Please call as soon as it's convenient." I have no idea what this may be about, but my unkind instinct is to assume that whatever Bernadette wants, it'll require time and energy that I'd prefer to spend elsewhere. But I have to acknowledge that (a) she's a good person and (b) strange as it seems to me, I have more in common with her than with most other colleagues. Yes, Bernadette, I'll call you back. But not right now.

The fourth one is addressed to Maureen, from someone speaking rapidly in French; it's Philippe, the guy from the francophone organization that Maureen used to work for. I have no hope of understanding what he's saying, but there's an urgency in his tone, as though he's warning her of some impending catastrophe. But what could it be? Or perhaps I'm wrong, and he's telling her about the failure of his previously-thought-to-be ideal relationship. Another minor mystery. He leaves a phone number at the end of his spiel, so I could call him—he speaks perfectly good English—and explain why Maureen will not be calling him back right away, as he seems to be imploring her to do. But I don't want to do that right now either.

In fact what I want to do is disappear into my study and immerse myself in the work of Richard Karp, something which could be construed as either escaping from reality, or, as I think on my more optimistic days, entering a superior one in which I can be pleasurably lost for hours at a time. But then I realize that, if I do that, and fail to contact Gene Brazil until, say, tomorrow, there could be trouble. He's probably waiting by his phone, hoping I'll miss his unspecified deadline for responding, so that he can send a couple of police cars, sirens screaming, lights pulsating, to track me down.

He picks up on the first ring. "Hugh Norman," I say, apprehensively.

"*Dr.* Norman, I presume," he shouts, obviously delighted to be able to deliver this witticism. Aren't detectives who've been working day and night to solve a crime supposed to be tired and short-tempered? "How are you, sir?" he goes on, adding, with what seems unnecessary emphasis: "Wha?"

"I'm, er, well, thanks. How can I help you?"

"Well, there's one or two details I'd like to ask you about. In person, if you don't mind."

"Of course not. I mean, I don't mind. I'd be happy to. Should I come in?" Better to co-operate, I'm thinking. I have nothing to hide, nothing to hide...."

"Come in?" This has struck him as a preposterous idea. "No, no, you don't need to come *in*, sir. Wha? No. I was thinking maybe I could come by your house for a minute or two. Tomorrow morning? Maybe around ten? If you can tear yourself away from, what is it, 'writing about books,' for a few minutes."

"I think I can do that," I say, bogusly jovial. Implicit in my tone, I hope, is the suggestion that I too have come to the conclusion that writing about books is absurd.

"Good, good. See you tomorrow, then."

"But can you give me some idea of what you want to ask me?"

He doesn't answer immediately. I can picture Brazil leaning back in his chair, squinting at the fluorescent light above his desk, perhaps rubbing his brow, considering whether to give me a serious answer—"We think you know a lot more than you're telling us, bozo"—or just to tell me to shut up and wait.

"I'd rather surprise you," he says finally. Then he laughs. "Just kidding, Dr. Norman. Wha? Don't worry about it, sir. See you soon. Take care, now." Is he chuckling as he hangs up?

What on earth does he want?

I call Raissa, but she isn't answering, so I leave a message saying I'd be delighted to escort her to Aaron Spracklin's show. Then it's into my study for the rest of the afternoon and late into the evening, emerging only for supper, and for a predictable visit from a certain neighbour.

The Richard Karp story I'm working on at the moment is about a man struggling to write a love poem for a woman who has no clue that he exists. Why he doesn't approach her is never made clear. The narrative focus is on his attempt to invent the language that he needs to make his vision seem real. But as he writes, he finds that every image, every turn of phrase somehow transmutes itself into something that speaks of death, however subtly. The woman, the protagonist's neighbour, glimpsed only occasionally by him, and almost always at a distance, is afflicted by a mysterious illness (there are sections narrated from her point of view) and ultimately dies. The protagonist learns of this after the fact, gives up his poem, attends her funeral, and then returns home to find that he can now write the poem as he had wanted to write.

The story exhibits a delicacy of touch that no critic I know of can explain or analyze convincingly. I'm left with the mundane task of writing something exegetical, feeling that I'm doing neither Karp nor the cause of criticism in general any favours. But still. It's something rather than nothing. I've managed to quote Kafka on parable, and make it seem relevant, at least to me. As I skim what I've written so far, I can see, maybe not a publishable article, but at least a conference paper taking shape. And yet.

The last conference paper I presented. Fifteen people in a nondescript classroom, bright Saturday morning sun streaming in, at least twelve of the fifteen hungover, perhaps two having read the story I was talking about, none having the tiniest granular fragment of interest in what I was saying about it. The moderator of the session (a cheerful Scot with whom I and a couple of others had shared a wee drap the night before) commenting, in a tone of mild admonition, that mine has been a "closely argued" presentation, meaning that it was too tedious for anyone to follow. There were no questions.

I recall the single-mindedness with which Cliff used to churn out such conference papers. Of course he'd maintain that he had some hope of impressing someone influential in a way that might lead to a tenure-track job, but in his heart he must have known that was a non-starter. We were a generation or two too late for that sort of thing to happen. But he insisted that he believed in the value of the content, no matter how arcane the topic. He was engaged in the search for truth, dammit, back in the days when at least some academics still believed in the notion of "truth." And he believed it was important for his attempts to discover truth to be communicated to others. That, I guess, is where we differ. My truth about Karp's fiction will be unlikely to be of interest to anyone else, just as Karp's fiction itself—with its own implicit but clear attempt to be "truthful"—is of interest to almost no one else.

Yes, a conference paper would earn me a free trip to somewhere—but certainly somewhere no more exotic than Halifax or Edmonton. And as I entertain this thought, I see Cliff's image, the young Cliff in his football jersey, brow wrinkling disapprovingly. *Was it for this?* No, Cliff, it wasn't. I dismiss his shade and set to work.

Eight in the evening and the doorbell. It's Andy Lawson of course, wittingly or not playing the role of the wacky next-door neighbour in a 1950s sitcom. And what if it is "wittingly?" What if he actually sees himself as playing a "role" in my life, or my and Maureen's? Bizarre questions, no doubt, but here I am asking them, though not out loud, as I reluctantly invite Andy to invade my space yet one more time. He cuts to the chase.

"Listen, Hugh, I need to tell you a bit more about Cynthia, about our relationship. Not about the abductee thing, in fact maybe you should just forget I told you that, and please don't bring it up when Cynthia is around. Okay?"

"Of course not. But really, your relationship is none of my business anyway, so maybe we should just—"

"No, no. I mean, we're friends, right? You're really my only friend in St. John's. Isn't it normal for friends to confide in each other about such things?"

"Would you like a drink?"

"Sure, I'll have a cup of tea or something."

This isn't quite what I had in mind, but anything to reduce the weird intensity I sense coming from him. "Let's go into the kitchen." (We've been awkwardly fumbling about in the front hallway.)

"The thing is," he says, and then stops. "Well, it's not just about my relationship with Cynthia."

"Okay."

He sits at the table. "I mean, when I met you and Maureen in St. Pierre, I couldn't help feeling there was something significant about it, that it wasn't a matter of chance."

"It was something of a coincidence, it's true." I'm trying to keep the tone neutral, as I put the kettle on. It's starting to occur to me that Andy may be experiencing some emotional distress, though he seems to be completely in control.

"Not really a coincidence, that's what I'm saying. It seems to be really important that we all saw that poster of the missing woman. You remember that." It's as though he's ordering me to remember, in the manner of a parody-Nazi: "You *vill* remember! Vee haf ways."

"Of course."

"There was something so sad and innocent about her. Don't you think?"

"Yes, you're right."

"And I could see that you and Maureen responded to that. It struck a chord, didn't it?"

"Yes. Yes, it did."

"So I guess my point here is, and this is what I want to convey to you, as a friend, is that when I first met Cynthia, I thought of her as being sort of like the woman on the poster."

I'm starting to feel a bit uncomfortable about the general drift here. Will he expect me to produce a similarly intimate account of my meeting Maureen? I decide to go for levity. "You don't mean that you think the woman on the poster was abducted by aliens? Or by the US government?" I add quickly, recalling the MILABS.

He looks confused. "No. No, that's not what I think."

"Sorry."

"No need to apologize. And even Cynthia is not a hundred per cent sure she's been abducted. It could all be fantasy. But it seems so real to her. It's as though she's the connecting point between two parallel universes, she says. I can't imagine what that would be like. Though maybe love is like that too, don't you think?"

"How do you mean?"

"There's you and the person you love. And then there's you and the rest of the world."

The kettle is boiling, which gives me the opportunity to back off. "Do you take sugar?"

"No thanks. Just milk. But to get back to the poster. I know this woman doesn't look anything like Cynthia, so you're probably wondering why she reminds me of her."

"Right. I wish I could offer you a biscuit or something, but I'm afraid—"

He cuts me off mid-sentence. "It has to do with Cynthia's foot."

What? At last, Andy's secret life revealed. A foot-fetishist! Somewhat banal, but still, it's something rather than nothing.

"I can see you're surprised. My mention of Cynthia's foot. But it has nothing to do with sexual attraction. It has to do with love."

"I see."

"I'm not sure that you do. The circumstances are unimportant, but the first thing I noticed about Cynthia, or more precisely, before I had any notion of who Cynthia was, I became aware of her foot. Her bare foot. Right foot. What struck me was the innocence of the foot. Of course you could say that about feet generally, I suppose. The innocence and the vulnerability, and with it an aura, I think that's word, an aura of sadness. Like the woman in that poster, even though you couldn't see her feet."

He's waving his spoon while staring at me, or "fixing his gaze" at me or on me, demanding eye contact.

"Think about the foot," he instructs me. "It has a job to do, essential but taken for granted. Where is its joy? It can't experience orgasm, for example. Nor can it think for itself, solve problems, dream dreams, have visions. Yet it's there, humble, obedient. It will go where it's told. Except in extreme circumstances. Does it delight in responding to the commands of its master, as angels are said to do? Is there a sense of satisfaction when it successfully follows the order to step forward? Who knows? The point is, all of this came to mind when I saw the foot, the foot that turned out to be connected to Cynthia, that was part of Cynthia. Do you see what I mean?"

Andy Lawson, junior executive in the oil industry. Who are you? Who the hell are you?

Tempting as it is, I will not blurt out something about Maureen's thighs.

Maureen phones around midnight, though of course it's well before midnight in Saskatchewan. She's ducked out of

AN EXILE'S PERFECT LETTER

a party, eight tipsy poets, she says, having a fun evening. She's having a wonderful time generally, she's been meeting some great people, she's been inspired to write some exciting new stuff. In the midst of this, I blurt something about having found a corpse. At first she thinks I'm joking. When I've convinced her that I'm telling the truth, I have to struggle to make her believe that the experience has not been "traumatic," and that really, things are pretty much as bland as usual. Am I lying? I don't want to spoil her evening, or her time at the retreat. Hoping to amuse, I give her the scoop on Andy and Cynthia, and the story of Cynthia's foot. That seems to work. And she sounds pleased when I tell her about the beard. Still, I haven't told her the whole truth. But I'm not sure how to do that.

Morning, and when I come downstairs, Foley is in the kitchen, making himself at home with orange juice and cereal—not that I begrudge him that, but I wish he wouldn't keep saying he will "remunerate" me as soon as a number of improbable finance-related events come to pass. He's either come in very late or spent the night elsewhere. I decide not to ask.

He does have a piece of news for me. The identity of the murder victim has been revealed.

Leonard Churchill.

I've heard the name before. I think.

"You developed this information through reliable sources?"

Foley looks slightly chagrined. "Actually I heard it on the radio. Before you got up."

"I see. Was there any further information?"

"The implication was that it was a drug deal gone bad. If you'll pardon the cliché. Though why they'd be doing a drug deal in the woods is a mystery. In any case this Churchill fellow was 'known to the police.'"

"Anything else?"

"That was about it."

I tell him that Detective Brazil will be back soon. "I'm starting to feel like Raskolnikov."

"Who?"

Despite myself, I start explaining who Raskolnikov is. Why did that name pop into my head? After all, I'm innocent. I didn't murder a female pawnbroker and her sister. Brazil is no Porphyry. And I don't think of myself as being above the law, do I?

Foley is intrigued. "So you have some sort of free-floating guilt that irrationally attaches itself to—"

"Yes, Foley. I know it's irrational. Much of what I feel is irrational."

Have I spoken too sharply? Foley looks confused, seems to be searching for the right thing to say, then decides not to say anything. He turns away, pours water into the kettle, flicks the switch.

"Leonard Churchill. Does that name mean anything to you?"

Foley looks relieved that he's being consulted rather than attacked. His brow furrows somewhat theatrically before he answers. "Can't say that I do. Should I?"

"It's just that I've heard it before. Can't say where, though."

"A former student, perhaps."

"Possibly. Did they say how old he was?"

"Can't remember."

Churchill is a common enough name in these parts. I must have had at least a dozen in various classes over the years, probably more. Apparently none has been distinctive enough for me to remember—though (it comes back to me now) there was one who was convinced that assigning an essay on the Frost sonnet "Design" was an attempt on my part to convert him to atheism. No amount of propaganda for godlessness was about to shake his faith, he let me know. But that was around fifteen years ago. Who knows what challenges to his faith he's encountered since.

But now I've got "Design" in my head, that sly little parable about the white spider and the white moth on the white flower, and what that confluence of whitenesses suggests about the structure of a world in which the innocent are consumed by the predatory. And I wonder whether some notion of design pertains to my current situation, what sinister force drew me to the spot where Leonard Churchill lay, like some craftily inert spider, to disrupt my orderly moth-ish life. And is Gene Brazil trying to miscast *me* in the role of spider, part of some grandiose dark pattern? If design govern in a thing so small.

If it did, Richard Karp would discern it. But I don't have his gift.

And then it hits me. In a Karp story published in the sixties a secondary-school teacher is falsely accused of murdering one of his students, whose body is found in the woods not far from the school. The teacher is badgered by an obnoxious detective, who is also annoyingly well-read, and explicitly compares himself to Porphyry and the teacher to Raskolnikov. But finally the detective becomes convinced of the teacher's innocence. The teacher then confesses. The detective doesn't believe him and keeps trying to find the real killer, but fails. The teacher is convicted on the basis of his confession, though there's no forensic evidence. He makes no attempt to recant, having come to believe he's serving some higher purpose, a belief sustained by certain ambiguous visionary—or psychotic—experiences. At the moment the verdict is read, he feels a sense of triumph. The story ends there.

The murdered student's name is Leonard Churchill.

An absolutely meaningless coincidence whose existence will distract me until, probably, Alzheimer's takes over.

I explain this to Foley as best I can.

"So life imitates art," he observes. "But really, what significance can it possibly have? It's not as though this Karp guy is a prophet or anything, right?" There's just the faintest undertone of anxiety in the question: has old Hugh gone off the deep end, he's wondering.

"It would be odd for someone publishing a story around 1968 to predict the name of a murder victim in 2006, wouldn't it? What would be the point?"

"So the only thing connecting these two events is the fact that you're aware of them?"

"Well, of course you're aware of them now too."

He flinches, as though I'm suggesting that he's agreed to join me in some dangerous, possibly illegal enterprise. "But they don't mean anything to me."

"They don't mean anything to me either. They're a challenge to my assumptions about meaningfulness. Are they part of some larger pattern I can't see, let alone understand?" I can sense Foley's unease. He knows that there's a "larger pattern," and that it can be discerned via Marxism. But part of him knows that's not the whole story, the part of him that wrote poetry and did the English-Literature half of his double major. He's been resisting recognizing that part of himself for a long time. So when someone else's hypothesized non-Marxist "larger pattern" erupts into conversation, he must feel a certain anxiety. His lips twist themselves into the semblance of a smile.

"It's okay, you can laugh."

"I'm not laughing."

"It's just that we have two facts whose relation seems to demand that there be some sort of, well, some sort of *meaning* involved. But there isn't."

Foley's face relaxes. I'm not going to go all wacky-visionary on him. "Perhaps," he says, "you should tell our detective friend about it. Maybe he'll have a theory. I'm joking, of course."

"Of course. You're a man of infinite jest, Foley."

I can picture Gene Brazil's face screwing up (as they say) as he tries to grasp the point that some guy almost forty years ago used the name "Leonard Churchill" in a story, that I am one of a very small number of people who now have any interest in this story (possibly the only one), and that I therefore regard it as uncanny—would he know the word "uncanny?"—that I am the person to have discovered the corpse of our very own Leonard Churchill.

"Much as I'd like to hang around to see how this plays out," Foley says.

"You have an important engagement elsewhere."

"Yes." He hesitates. "But I may be seeing you later, in fact. Are you going to Aaron Spracklin's show, by any chance? I'm going to be reviewing it for the CBC." How Foley manages to get these commissions has always baffled me. He has no qualifications as a theatre critic. I suspect some sort of erotically tinged connection with a female producer, but Foley is always evasive when I press him for detail.

"Yes. I am."

"I assumed as much. Always supportive of your ex-students, aren't you?"

"Actually he isn't an ex-student of mine. But he's a friend of Raissa."

"Right. Raissa McCloskey. I think she was somewhat attracted to me once upon a time, but unfortunately nothing ever came of it." He stops for a moment, and his eyes glaze, as though he's imagining what might have come of it; then, with an effort, he hauls himself back to reality. "In any case. I just wanted you to be prepared. I expect to be accompanied."

"Yes?" This is unusual. Why does he think I need to be "prepared"?

"You know Anna Walmsley? The painter? You may recall I had a brief, uh, relationship with her a few years back."

"Yes, I recall." Quite clearly, as it happens. Nutty as the proverbial fruitcake, Anna Walmsley was, and presumably still is, the archetypal artist-from-the-mainland who comes to Newfoundland, imposes her enthusiastic ignorance of the place on everything in sight, and is somehow able to establish herself as someone whose work is worth paying attention to—although not everyone is on board with that last bit. The *Telegram* review of her latest show (*Dreams of the Icebergs*) included the unkind assertion that "Ms. Walmsley is possessed by the terrible energy of mediocrity," the review written by none other than my colleague

Bernadette O'Keefe. Anna's affair with Foley lasted less than two weeks, characterized as it was by, he said, her insufferable flakiness (though it was she who ended it, making him temporarily homeless). I met her only once, a drunken evening with Foley at the Ship, when she dominated the conversation with a series of rambling narcissistic monologues, much to our amusement, at least for a while. And now?

"Well," Foley says, "it will perhaps come as a surprise, given the unhappy *denouement* of our previous..." He's groping for a word, recognizing now that "relationship" is perhaps too grandiose a term to deploy in this context. Finally he gives up. "Well, we're back together. Sort of. Provisionally. Not"—he says, raising a hand to forestall my interjection—"that cohabitation is imminent. One step at a time. I trust that I may continue to prevail upon your hospitality until Maureen returns."

"Trust away. But I seem to remember that, back when, you were judged to be both a potential rapist and an unfit potential father. Have you been granted a pardon?"

"She speculates that her perception was skewed by some sort of hormonal imbalance. All is pretty much forgiven." He hesitates again. "I really must be off."

It's still only nine-thirty and Brazil isn't due until ten, so I decide to call Bernadette, since (worst case scenario) I can use Brazil's arrival as a reason to end the conversation, if it goes that long.

"What I'm thinking, Hugh," Bernadette says, "is that, since we're both concerned about the direction of the department" [we are?], "perhaps we could make common cause and gather support for what we think the direction should be. I'm sure there are others who think as we do."

It would seem rude of me to ask what, exactly, she thinks that "we" think, though I have a good general idea. But I'd rather not go directly there, so I keep quiet, though it's obvious that she's expecting me to say something.

"Hugh? You did get that copy of Lister's article I sent you by internal mail?"

"Yes. I did."

"Well. Doesn't it represent everything we despise about current trends in scholarship? The triviality, the over-ingeniousness, the attempt to make much of little? And then there's that ridiculous 'ludic narrative' thesis he's going to supervise."

This is getting to be a bit much. "So you want to start a campaign to get rid of Lister? But that would be"—and here I pause, because the phrase I want to utter, "batshit crazy," would be inappropriate—"that would be unlikely to happen. As you must know," I add hastily, lest she be offended by my no doubt patronizing tone.

"No, Hugh. That's not what I had in mind." She's become a bit impatient now. "It's not Lister himself that's the problem. We're large enough to accommodate a Lister in our midst. It's rather the Listerization of the department that worries me, the collective abdication of our role as curators of what's truly valuable in our discipline. You know what I'm talking about."

And of course I do. But it's a lost cause, perhaps well lost, I'm beginning to think. "So what do you propose?"

"Well, I think we should draft a sort of charter of the basic principles that the graduate studies committee should follow, and try to have it adopted as the official position of the department. With clear definitions of what constitutes valid research. And what doesn't. It would be a gesture, Hugh, a gesture in the direction of sanity. As opposed to where we're going now. So what do you think?"

I'm thinking a variety of uncharitable thoughts. "What are the chances of getting enough support?"

An exasperated sigh. "Hugh, it's the *principle* that's important, not whether we'd succeed. But you understand that. I'd really like you to help me draft something. Before you say no, please give it some thought."

"Okay. I'll do that."

Gene Brazil beams at me as I open the door for him, though there are bags under his eyes.

"Good to see you again, sir. Wha?"

I back away from the door to let him in. He's carrying a large manila envelope, which he waves at me in weary jubilation.

"I think we got 'er cracked, sir. Just a couple questions for you."

I usher him into the kitchen. He sits down, sighing, puts the envelope on the table.

"So you've had some success, detective?"

He stares at me. "Oh, we know who did it, if that's what you mean."

I'm almost ready to ask him *Was it me?* Instead I say, "And how can I help you?"

"By telling me the truth, sir." This is accompanied by a sort of manic cackle, which may or may not have been deliberately manufactured. "I don't want to waste time, Dr. Norman. When you were at Long Pond, walking around, did you see any one of these guys?" And here he pulls several photographs out of the envelope he's been carrying and plunks them down in front of me.

Of course one of them is Mr. Don't-fuck-with-me.

There's a split second when I consider lying. After all, when I saw him on the path it was at a point where, if I'd come along thirty seconds later, I would never have seen him. He would have taken the side path to the university parking lot, no doubt his escape route. But the fact is, I'm afraid to lie. Gene Brazil is Authority, and I'm...what? "A Canadian" would be the easy answer, but so is Rex Nairn, and I have no doubt what he'd say. Cliff MacIntyre wouldn't lie, though. And now I recognize with sudden conviction that it's not really a matter of fear, but rather a question of self-definition. Am I the sort of person who lies to avoid inconvenience in such a serious matter? How tawdry that would be, how demeaning. Of course that sort of conviction may be rooted in self-deceit, but still.

"Yes, I saw this guy. On the path at the west end of the pond."

Brazil nods, smiles. "You'd be able to testify to that in court, would you, sir?"

"Yes. I would."

He relaxes, and so do I. It wasn't me after all.

TWELVE

Rex and I meet at The Ship an hour before Aaron Spracklin's show. (Rex is going too, his ticket booked well in advance, someone from the magazine arranging it long-distance.) He's very pleased with his interview with Zachary Philip Dwyer. "You're right," he says, "he *is* the voice of the dispossessed, the disenfranchised, the outcast, and so forth. His very existence is a stinging rebuke to the bourgeois power structure that seeks to silence him. Pretty good, hey?"

"Not that it's pretentious or anything."

"Of course it is. But it's *good* pretentious. Just what my editors want—the Newfoundland artist as primitive, raw, fifty years out of fashion. I can build the whole article around him. The anti-Canadian thing goes over well, too. No matter how many Ottawa bureaucrats try to bribe him to celebrate Canada Day, he'll resist in the name of the brave men who died at Beaumont-Hamel. Exactly the sort of thing

I'm looking for, that quaint fierceness or fierce quaintness or whatever it is."

"Did he say how many bureaucrats have actually approached him?"

"I didn't ask. But he implied there were hordes."

"You do understand that many people here see him for what he is. And that if you focus on him, you'll be downplaying or ignoring the real artists."

"And my readers will neither know nor care. I'm making art myself here, Hugh, designing a product perfectly calibrated for what it has to do. The real artists can take care of themselves. In the long run they always do. You know that. In the meantime, this guy can be a poster boy for the flashy bullshit people relate to."

"Cliff wouldn't have approved." Spoken as if in jest, but where the hell did that come from?

Rex sips from his pint. "Cliff, yes, that icon of integrity."

Unkind, but I bite my tongue. Misguided Cliff may have been, but there are things he would have refused, out of ornery allegiance to principle. Rex, in my reading of him at least, has never seemed to have had that problem.

He reads my silence. "Too harsh? But from what you've said, there was something, what, *unbending* about him. As an adult. And that's how I remember him in the old days, too."

Except, it just now occurs to me, there's something correspondingly inflexible about Rex himself, though much harder to pin down than in Cliff's case, not connected to any recognizable principle but to some obscure self-concept that mustn't be questioned or modified.

"Yes, I guess it's true he was unbending. For good or ill."

"Well." Time to move on, he means.

And we do. I end up telling him about the two Leonard Churchills, the fictional and the brutally factual.

He looks puzzled.

And I realize there's something intrinsically silly about my fixation on this random fact. Why should I think there's something significant going on here? Why do I think at some level that my life will have the coherence of a well-made short story, every detail carefully selected for aesthetic effect?

"So it's an odd coincidence, but I don't really see..."

"Yes, you're right, let's change the subject."

"But this interests me, as a glimpse into your psychology. It's somehow important for you to see this as meaningful, as part of a pattern, right? Why is that?"

We're back in high school, and he knows something I don't—about football, girls, poetry, it hardly matters. He's sensed a weakness, and he's determined to exploit it. Whatever I come up with, whatever nugget of insight I may have will be politely received and quietly dismissed as something that had perhaps fleetingly occurred to him and as quickly been rejected.

"I'm professionally committed to finding meaning everywhere" is the best I can dredge up.

"I'm more about *creating* meaning," he says, in a tone suggesting parody of one-upmanship but in fact conveying something more like "How fruitless is this enterprise, [subtext] how much nobler is my approach than yours."

"You mean, as in investing Zachary Philip Dwyer with spurious significance to make your article sexier?"

"Well, that's a crude example, but yes, I have a goal in mind and I do what needs to be done. Now in your case you seem to think that life or fate or something has designed this situation for you, and it's up to you to figure it out, to *read* it. But maybe you should ask what you *want* it to mean, because it's obvious you want to find something there. So decide what it is and impose your own meaning on it."

"Simple as that?"

He's not sure if I'm being sarcastic, then decides I shouldn't be, so I'm not. He permits himself a minor grin. "Yep."

In some ways we haven't changed in fifty (count 'em) years. I'm wondering if maybe he's right, as I've always wondered, before deciding he isn't.

But really, what navel-gazing. I oughta be ashamed.

Still, two Leonard Churchills. What are the odds?

Our pints drained, we move across Duckworth and up the steps to the LSPU Hall, where we join the crowd in the ground-floor gallery area. Raissa spots us immediately. I've ascertained that she hasn't been on Rex's list of potential interviewees, and I want to make sure she gets a chance to charm or bully her way on to it. (What happened to my earlier feeling of possessiveness? Three words, the last of which is "Dwyer." I'd love to see her upstage him in Rex's piece.) After the introduction, I insist on getting us all a drink, in order to give her a clear shot. As I'm insinuating myself into the crush at the bar, someone taps me on the shoulder. It's Foley, female companion in tow. But she stays in the background.

"Just want to alert you," Foley says, bending close to my ear. "Your friend from the Constab is on the scene. Look to your left."

So I do, and there, sure enough, is Gene Brazil, admiring, or pretending to admire a small painting. Can he really be relentlessly tracking my every move, waiting for the moment when I betray my non-existent guilt? Perhaps, despite what he's told me, he suspects that I'm somehow implicated in the demise of Leonard Churchill. And that charade with the photograph: perhaps the real intent was to confirm that I know Mr. Don't-fuck-with-me, my partner in crime. But then why would I admit to having recognized him? ("These guys always outsmart themselves....") I turn back to Foley, who, apparently sensing the distress in my expression, tries to lighten things up.

"Maybe he thinks you'll lead him to another body," he suggests.

"Thank you, Foley."

"I think you've met Anna," he says, rolling his eyes in memory of the evening four years ago when I *did* meet Anna at the height—or depth—of his brief affair with her, and she revealed herself to be the Queen of Too Much Information, leaving both us guys shamefully amused. I hope she's forgotten about it.

"Actually, I don't think we have," she says, smiling demurely.

"Nice meeting you," I say, and then, to Foley, "Thanks for the heads-up."

By the time I've emerged from the bar-scrum with our beers, Brazil seems to have vanished. I wonder if perhaps he's here simply to enjoy the show. Why shouldn't a detective be a theatregoer? Or maybe his wife has dragged him here. No need to assume the worst. No need at all.

When I've made my way back to Rex and Raissa, they've long since made arrangements for the interview. Raissa is pressing him for personal details. Married? Kids? The last book he's read? He really knew Hugh when you guys were kids? What was Hugh like? There's no end to her appetite for this sort of thing, and it's fun to watch Rex try to fend her off. He's obviously relieved when it's time to move upstairs for the performance.

A Man Alone in a Room turns out to be a brilliant piece of theatre. Aaron Spracklin's monologue is witty and urbane, but with an undercurrent of something dark. The stage is almost bare, the set rudimentary—a room in a house somewhere in downtown St. John's, with windows on three sides. There's a chair, a table, a refrigerator, a bed, but Spracklin's main prop is a pair of binoculars, which he uses to scan the outside world. But occasionally, with oddly comic effect, he uses them to peer into a mirror while commenting on his life in apparently spontaneous, but probably tightly controlled stream-of-consciousness.

The premise is that he's rented the room sight unseen. His first action is to measure it, concluding that it's slightly smaller than advertised and establishing his character as obsessive and not entirely sympathetic. He's an outsider to the city, but he's lived here for some time, years perhaps. He knows many people, some of whom he spies on with his binoculars. Speaking to an unseen listener (who may be no one other than himself), he explores the nooks and crannies of his consciousness. A major strand of the narrative involves his infatuation with an unnamed woman who once seemed unattainable but then became his lover, and now, for reasons that Spracklin's character can't seem to fathom, has rejected him. It may be for that reason that he has rented the room, a retreat from the "real" world. But the storyline is to some extent obscured by his quirky comments on a variety of unrelated topics, some mundane (how to prepare a meal of caplin), some abstruse (the philosophical implications of wormholes). There's a lot of slapstick, too, as he blunders around the room, lanky and seemingly uncoordinated, but sometimes surprisingly graceful in a lugubrious, long-faced, long-jawed sort of way.

On a couple of occasions, the binoculars are directed at the audience, with a disconcerting yet laugh-provoking effect, as if each of us individually is being cruelly exposed to his all-seeing gaze, and yet we're also meant to enjoy the satisfaction he was deriving from forcing us to experience such exposure. There's much commentary on the Irving Oil tanks on the Southside Hills (all too visible from one of his windows), a metaphor for something not clearly defined but certainly negative. And there's something Beckett-like about the way that wit, passion, and psychological insight are cobbled together to prevent some final revelation of absurdity. Or is the point that the character embraces absurdity and invites the audience to do so as well? And yet the whole piece is suffused, paradoxically, with apparently unwarranted good humour.

When it's over, there's a standing ovation. As he takes his bows, I look around to see if I can spot Brazil, but I can't. I also wonder if my former research interest, the man who was once Father Alphonsus Cleary, is present in his new avatar. Although Cleary is no longer on my scholarly radar, I'm still intrigued by the question of how he has defined himself in his supposedly posthumous state. Given the connection between him and Aaron Spracklin, it's reasonable to assume that, if he's still alive, he's here tonight. But I have no clue what he might look like.

Minutes later, we're back at The Ship, Raissa and Rex, and I, Raissa now lobbying on Aaron's behalf. Surely Rex would want to interview him, too?

"The thing is," Rex says, "he's too sophisticated for my purposes. This magazine I'm writing for wants Newfoundland to be earthy, simple. Your Aaron doesn't fit the picture the way, say, Zachary Philip Dwyer does. No subtlety there, and that's a good thing, as far as my editors are concerned."

"We're supposed to be naive rustic folk," Raissa says evenly.

"Yes," Rex says, not missing the irony exactly but taking it into account and deciding to ignore it. "Drinking and screwing, as in, what is it, *Up to Me Arse in Muck*. That's the sort of thing my readers want to hear about Newfoundland."

"What if that's not what Newfoundland wants to say to them?"

"Well, that's another matter entirely, isn't it?" Rex says genially. "Newfoundland—whatever that means in this context—can say whatever it likes. The question is, 'Who's going to listen?' Now take this performance tonight. Powerfully imagined, impeccably delivered. But frankly, so what? This Spracklin guy is based in Toronto now, anyway, isn't he? Forget St. John's, it could've been set anywhere, could've been Toronto for that matter."

"Toronto, that mecca of subtlety."

"Very witty, Hugh, but one thing about Toronto—"

And here Rex interrupts himself, looks over my shoulder. I turn around. Two people have been hovering behind me. Of course it's Foley and Anna.

"May we join you?" Foley asks. He's begging, and I can see what's happened: Foley has told Anna about Rex and his article, and Anna wants to get in on the action. I can't turn him away.

Anna's tangly dark hair seems to explode from her head. It flows below her shoulders like black lava. Her breasts seem determined to escape from her colourful top. I do my best to avert my eyes.

Five minutes later, Anna has Rex at her mercy, much to Foley's embarrassment and Raissa's and my amusement.

"...show is called *Dreams of the Icebergs*? Because I think of icebergs as sentient beings, I mean when they break off from glaciers we call it 'calving,' right? So we naturally think of them as animals, so I thought, well, as they're floating down from Greenland or wherever, they don't have much to do, I mean an iceberg can't *do* anything, right, except literally go with the flow, so if they *were* sentient, they'd probably just sort of relax and fall asleep and dream. But then what would they dream about? Coming from Ontario I really had no idea about iceberg psychology, so I asked around here and got mostly funny looks from people in the arts community, they're slow to accept outsiders, although some *are* accepting and I've had a couple of shows before this one, *Ghosts of the Cod* was my first, I think it's good when some of these traditional Newfoundland subjects are given a fresh look by somebody who's maybe not as set in their ways as a lot of artists here are.

"...anyway, the whole idea of the sexual aspect came from me trying to put myself in the place of these icebergs, I mean if we're thinking of them as living creatures they couldn't just be dreaming of other icebergs because then the painting would just be of an iceberg with like a different iceberg in a sort of cartoon bubble above it, so I was thinking that it'd be natural for a person to have sexual thoughts while they're floating southward, I mean the water would be getting warmer, comparatively, and sexier, so that gave me the idea of juxtaposing the image of the iceberg, which can be quite sexual-looking itself in certain ways, with the images of people involved in various kinds of sexual activity, which has turned out to be sort of controversial here.

"…of course inspired by some of my own relationships, I mean there are people who think they can identify themselves in the paintings and some of them are quite upset but I think in most cases they should be flattered, I mean I wasn't out to make anyone look worse than they actually are, although some of the depictions are pretty accurate and unflattering, and there's been one review where the woman actually used the word 'cruel,' but that was because the guy in question is now with her, right, and she thought it was unfair because even though I didn't show his face, there were certain marks on parts of his body that one or two people recognized, so I've been unfairly badmouthed for that because word gets around here pretty quickly, especially if the word has something to do with gossip."

Foley, who has been making a number of attempts to attract Anna's attention, finally succeeds.

"…Terry's anxious to go, I see, he wants to get to work on his review, so I can't go into detail on the individual pieces, but anyway, bottom line, the task of the artist isn't to be popular but to stand up for what she believes in, right? Hope you can use some of this in your article. And you'll come to see the show, right. The information's all on this flyer. And here, I'll give you my card and you can call me whenever you like. Day or night, haha. I'll make myself available, promise."

<hr>

It's later, the others have gone, I'm alone at the table. I don't do this often, but tonight I wanted another pint before trudging homeward up the hill. And then Aaron Spracklin sits down, and with him a man I've never seen before, looking about seventy, bespectacled, balding, tufts of gray over his ears. Inquisitive eyes, classic Irish-influenced facial features. He looks happy. He's smiling.

"We meet again," Aaron says.

I start to say some obvious things about the performance, but he cuts me off, gestures toward the other man.

"And we meet for the first time," says the companion. I know who he must be.

"This is the world's leading authority on the novels of Alphonsus Cleary," Aaron tells him. "And this man needs no introduction, does he, Dr. Norman?"

Of course he doesn't. He's my scholarly obsession of years past, and as we smile politely at each other, I realize he's no longer of much interest to me. Four years ago I would have been honoured to meet him, the subject of my ridiculously obsessive academic labour. But now, the monograph completed, published, and—as predicted—ignored, I feel close to indifferent. Yes, his novels are imaginative and distinctive and deserve a wider audience. But so do the books of countless other worthy, unknown writers. Yes, his work did speak to me in a particularly striking way at a certain time in my life, but that time is gone. So I'm reduced to dealing with him as I would any other stranger I might meet in a bar.

There's amusement in his expression as we shake hands. Perhaps he's intuiting my thoughts.

"I understand that you wanted to meet me."

"I did, but that was several years back. And I'm honoured, of course. But then I had a bunch of questions that needed answering. But now, not so much."

"I'm an anticlimax."

"Something like that. No offense. I mean, according to Aaron back then, your advice was that I should focus on the novels and forget about trying to connect them to your life. So I did that, as best I could. And that work is done now. I've moved on."

"Admirable."

"The thing that interests me now," I say, realizing it only as I speak, "is the idea that your former self died."

"Yes, well, I needed a clean break."

"But why fake your death? That was hardly necessary."

"Yes, it's true that many priests at that time were leaving the Church in more conventional ways. But I didn't want the fuss, the confrontations, the bureaucratic rigmarole. I wanted a new name, new everything. To be born again, if that's not too pretentious. And even if it is."

"But you made sure that Aaron knew who you were."

"Yes, among others. Fabian O'Callaghan, for example. But of the younger generation, the artistic ones, I chose Aaron. I wanted that connection to local tradition, that it be present at some level, however deeply buried. Egotism, no doubt."

"And so you stopped writing, too?"

Cleary hesitates, takes a swig of his pint. "You know," he says, "the history of literature gives us very few examples of writers who knew when to shut up. But I'm one of them.

I'd had my say. I didn't care that there was no one listening. I'd just come to the end of it. Rimbaud had the right idea. Nineteen years old and he saw he'd gone as far as he could go. So why pretend, why lie? Why not head off to Africa and do a bit of gun-running?"

"But as a new person, couldn't you have some new things to say?"

Cleary smiles and drinks, seeming to imply that the question is too naïve to deserve an answer. But it's not a no.

Aaron interjects: "You're not going to ask about his current identity?"

"No, and not because I know you guys won't tell me. It just really doesn't matter to me." And it's true. I'm surprised at how little I care about whoever Cleary is now.

"Excellent," Cleary says. "And what does matter?"

"Well, an old friend died recently. I found a dead body the other day. And, although this is almost too trivial to mention, the name of the dead man is the same as the name of a character in a story that I've been writing about. The character died too. I'm obsessed with this coincidence or synchronicity or whatever it is. I know all about the tendency to find patterns where there aren't any. Nevertheless. Do you know what I mean?"

"I do," says Cleary or post-Cleary. "But it's nothing. Forget about it."

"So there's no profundity lurking here, nothing significant about this fact that connects fiction with the real world?"

"Sorry, but that's bullshit."

"Is that what Alphonsus Cleary would say?"

"No, but he's dead."

"And your advice would be?"

"Get over it. It's a random conjunction of events, nothing more."

There's been something claustrophobic about this whole encounter, a sense that my world is somehow constricting. The Cleary I've discerned from the novels—witty, acerbic, passionate, fond of making reference to Jung—has been replaced by this unremarkable person, relaxed, bland but apparently happy in his new life, whatever it consists of.

And why do I need authority figures at my age, anyway?

"So," Aaron says, after a slightly uncomfortable silence. "What are you working on now, Dr. Norman?"

Aaron, of course, has never heard of Richard Karp. Cleary knows the name but hasn't read anything by him. I start to explain.

"A convert," Cleary interrupts. "Animated by excessive zeal, no doubt. I'm joking. Interesting, though, that you should be drawn to someone like that, after having written about, you know, Cleary. Now that should tell you more than this coincidence you've been obsessing over."

I realize that I've had enough for one evening. I'm not curious about what my interest in Karp "should tell" me. Maybe because it might tell me that I've wasted my life, am still wasting it. I stand up, maybe too abruptly, as both men look surprised. I have the sense that Aaron Spracklin is sizing me up as comic material. Cleary's expression morphs into something harder to read. Have I disappointed him? Perhaps his major critical interpreter should have been sharper, more insightful, more respectful?

We shake hands. "Nice meeting you," he says.

I climb the steps to Duckworth, and there (of course?) are Andy and Cynthia, apparently waiting for a cab. How did I not notice that they were in there with the rest of us?

"I could see you were busy with your friends," Cynthia says. "Andy, of course, was all for coming over and barging in, but I thought—"

"We did have a minor disagreement about that," Andy says. "I enjoy meeting new people. For the record, would you have minded?"

"Not at all," I lie. Andy, I suspect, would have found a way to dominate the conversation, in a spirit of genial innocence. Best to change the subject quickly. "So, can I share a cab with you guys?" I confess that I'm not looking forward to the hike up Long's Hill. Every year it seems to get a bit longer.

Of course I can join them.

"I very much enjoyed the show," Cynthia says, when we're in the cab, "although a lot of the local references were lost on me. What's up with Coleman's Grocery, for example? I mean that bit where he described the women cashing their welfare cheques seemed unnecessarily cruel. Was the point that Newfoundlanders have unhealthy diets?"

Andy: "I think it was more that these women were obviously living sad lives, and he wanted us to feel compassion for them."

Cynthia the abductee. I'd forgotten until now. She and Andy snuggle in the back seat; I'm in the front. We're waiting at the traffic light at the top of Long's Hill, the red that takes forever to change. We'd be sitting ducks if the aliens came after her now. The driver is unusually taciturn for a St. John's cabbie. I'm half-expecting him to break into an incomprehensible monologue for the amusement of the mainlanders.

Instead he says: "When the welfare cheques come in, I drive them home from Coleman's. I could tell you a thing or two about 'unhealthy diets.'" Then he shuts up.

A minute after the light turns green and we're all home. I insist on paying, my front-seat location giving me a crucial advantage over Andy, who struggles to get his wallet out of his pocket. Too late.

"You have to come in for a nightcap," he says. It sounds more like a command than an invitation.

"Yeah," Cynthia says, with more enthusiasm than I would have predicted. "Do come in."

So I do. First time I've been inside Andy's house, come to think of it.

"Everything's rented," Cynthia says, apparently by way of apologizing. "I can't wait until we live in the same place, in a real house with real furniture."

"This is good enough for the time being," Andy says. "Our real life will be elsewhere."

Andy produces a bottle, and the conversation rambles for a time. Then something happens. I see Andy beaming at her—there's no other word for it—he beams at her and then looks at me, and for a moment I'm inside what they have for each other, it's as real as the taste of the wine, and I stare down at Cynthia's right foot (she's kicked off her sandals), an ordinary functional workhorse of a foot, no hint of the erotic about it, and Andy catches my eye and nods, then winks, yes winks, and in short order I've said good-night, and I'm fumbling with my key, ready to enter the dark house next door.

THIRTEEN

Later, very late, on the phone with Maureen. Our dialogue less coherent than usual, since I've had so much to drink. I've got lots of material for her, the love story of Andy and Cynthia. She herself is having a great time. I get thumbnail descriptions of her new friends. They're all having fun writing villanelles, as an exercise. And then I'm telling her about the two Leonard Churchills. I actually feel annoyed with myself for doing this. Yes, I've told both Rex and Cleary, but this is somehow different, involving as it does a part of myself that I haven't revealed to Maureen, the part that hangs out in empty catacombs, drawing graffiti of mythical creatures on the walls. This must be my new, bare-faced persona.

After some back-and-forth centring on the fact that both Leonard Churchills have ended up dead, Maureen goes for the jugular: "Oh, so this is about your friend who died, is it?"

"No, it's not 'about' him, about Cliff." I'm staring out the kitchen window into the backyard. The outside light by the deck casts a semi-circle of unnatural brightness over the lawn, which needs to be mowed.

"Okay," she says, in the manner of someone humouring a child.

"I mean, do you really think it's about him?"

"Well, probably. If you think there's some kind of meaning, it must have something to do with death."

"Well, maybe it does."

"But here's my idea."

"What?"

"Well, we could get married. For example."

Some part of me has been expecting this for a good while. I'm not sure how to respond, though: "What would that change?" would sound churlish, as would "That seems rather drastic, doesn't it?" Tipsy though I am, I recognize that flippancy might be fatal.

So I say "We could."

"Affirmation of life over death, Hughie. Think about it."

"I will."

And I'm not averse to the idea. Life over death, indeed. Though we're well past the point of conceiving new life, and death will get us both in the end. But that's not what she means. Probably best not to push this any further at the moment, though. And Maureen seems to agree, as she says "We'll talk about it when I get back, okay?"

After some silliness we say goodnight, and I notice the TURP pamphlet on the counter by the sink. My own little *memento mori*. I haven't told Maureen about that. And I've forgotten to mention the phone message from Philippe.

Mid-morning and the phone wakes me. It's Gene Brazil. He'd like to "drop by" again, he says, but "nothing official" this time. He's sorry he didn't get a chance to talk to me at the Hall. That Aaron Spracklin is quite something, though, isn't he? Wha? So much for the idea that he was engaging in surreptitious surveillance. Or is it all a ploy to somehow throw me off guard? Sounds far-fetched. In any case, what choice do I have?

"Sure," I tell him, as groggily cheerful as I can manage. "Come on by." We agree on early afternoon. Shortly after this, Foley appears. He hasn't spent the night here. He's come to collect his stuff, Anna waiting for him in her car. He's buoyant, upbeat. "It's not going to be like last time," he assures me, unwarrantedly inferring skepticism on my part. Okay, maybe warrantedly. I recall that one of the reasons their previous connection disintegrated was that Anna thought Foley was a "potential rapist," a judgment based purely on intuition. Also that he would be an unfit father for her hypothetical child, not that he would dream of applying for that job.

"So what's changed?"

"Four years have passed. She no longer wants a child. Her career is everything, she says. And in relationships, she's come to understand the importance of compromise."

"Well. Good luck, then."

"I must run. We're off to the CBC so I can record my review of the Spracklin piece. It'll be on the afternoon show today, if you want to give it a listen. Written in some haste just after leaving that convivial gathering. It's sort of stream-of-consciousness, had to be, given my, er, domestic arrangements of yestereve. I'd be interested in your opinion. Should you happen to hear it."

"I'll do my best."

Gene Brazil arrives, smiling but somewhat diffidently, as though he's acknowledging that he's abdicated his authority. He's got a large manila envelope.

"Sorry to disturb you, Dr. Norman," he says. "This'll just take maybe five minutes of your time, okay?"

I invite him into the kitchen. He declines my offer of tea or coffee. He puts the envelope on the table. "I've come to ask a favour. This has nothing to do with the case. Wha?"

"What favour could I possibly do for you?"

"Well, Dr. Norman, I've done a bit of research on you. One of your areas of expertise is creative writing, is it not?"

"I don't know if I'd call it expertise, exactly. But."

"Yes, well, I've done my homework. You did see me at the Hall last night, didn't you? I bet that surprised you a bit, didn't it, sir?"

"No need to call me 'sir.'"

"Right. Dr. Norman. Hugh, if I may. The point I'm making here is that you probably thought, 'He's just a cop, who would've thought he'd be interested in the theatre.' Isn't that right, sir, Dr. Norman? Hugh?"

"No, no, not at all," I lie.

He snorts. "No need to lie. What else could you have thought? 'There's Gene Brazil, following me around?' That's paranoid territory. Our paths cross in two different contexts and you jump to a ridiculous conclusion? I don't think so. No, you've got more sense than that, don't you? So I think you probably had me pigeonholed as someone who, well, *shouldn't have been there*. Wha?"

"I admit, it was a bit of a surprise."

"You see? That's just human nature, right? But. People can be pretty complicated. Have different sides to them. Now in my case, I've always wanted to be a writer."

My heart sinks as I see where this is going. I can't help but glance at the envelope.

"Ah yes. The envelope. The envelope, please. Ha ha. Yes, the wonderful thing about writing, I think, is that anyone can be a writer. Doesn't require expensive equipment, or years of training, or anything like that. It's not like it's ballet or something, is it? Writing is no respecter of persons. Do I have that right, Hugh?"

"Yes, yes of course." Decades of academic wisdom behind that response. Yes, anyone can be a writer. Potentially.

"Dostoyevsky," he says reflexively, as he drags what is obviously a manuscript out of the envelope. It's disquietingly thick.

"Dostoyevsky?"

"My main inspiration. You've read him, of course, haven't you? I mean, not all of him, right? Who has? But you know, *Crime and Punishment, The Brothers Karamazov*, the major ones?"

"Yes, certainly."

"You remember the Grand Inquisitor scene?"

"Of course."

He's placed the manuscript on the table between us, slightly closer to me.

"You know, the Grand Inquisitor has this long song and dance about how people don't really want freedom, the freedom that Jesus promised them, that they wanted the Church to basically tell them what to do?"

"Yes."

"Well, see, I think one of the things Dostoyevsky is saying there is that anyone who creates something, like a novel, say, is like Jesus, on the side of freedom, see, and the Inquisitor, the guy who represents the elite, the powerful, he tries to crush creativity. Wha? Do you see what I'm saying?"

"Yes, I do."

"So for a long time I've been trying to get this published, and I keep running into brick walls. It's like the Inquisitor is running the publishing business in this country."

"It is very difficult to get a book published."

"So I'm wondering if maybe you could have a look at this, maybe make a few suggestions for improvement? I mean, you've got the expertise, and you seem to have a bit of free time now when you're not teaching. I'd be very grateful. Not that I could do anything about your parking tickets, ha ha."

"I could have a look at it, I suppose." How I hate myself. *I'm* the fucking Grand Inquisitor. Writing is not for amateurs. I represent an institution which, by exalting the achievements of the dead and famous, is expressly designed to discourage amateurs. It's an article of faith that the literary excrescences of amateurs are best kept unpublished, so they can't offend the educated gaze. On the other hand, I'm professionally committed to helping said amateurs as best I can.

"I know it looks a bit long," Brazil says, as if to imply that, while regrettable, this is a fact of nature that can't be altered. Also that the appearance of length may be some sort of optical illusion. "Four hundred and fourteen pages, to be exact. But it's double-spaced."

"What's it about?" Please don't let it be autobiographical. Please.

"Well, it's about a serial killer. Set in the nineteenth century. I'm a bit of a history buff, see. Late nineteenth century St. John's, around the time of the Great Fire. He's a sort of Jack the Ripper figure. People start turning up dead. The Constabulary gets taunting letters from the killer. And there's an intrepid detective, who...well, I don't want to spoil it for you, Hugh. If you could just skim through it, like, and tell me what you think."

"Yes. Well, it might take me some time." The guy has actually read Dostoyevsky. I will do it. Out of what warped sense of obligation?

"Of course. No hurry. No hurry at all."

Four hundred and fourteen pages.

"You've obviously put a lot of work into this."

"Yes," he says modestly. "A lot of research. Several drafts before I got this far. And something like eight rejections now."

What will I say to him, when I've done the "skimming?" What "improvements" will I be able to suggest?

"Were any of the rejections encouraging?"

"Not really. Form letters. It doesn't fit in with their plans. Nobody was rude, exactly. But."

"I know what you mean. Well, I'll see if I can come up with some suggestions."

And two minutes later, he's gone, after a firm handshake, a sadly ingratiating smile, and the information that for the last couple of years he's been hard at work on a sequel. I pick up the manuscript, check out a page or two. It's not as bad as I'd thought. Which makes things even worse, in a way.

Rex calls. His girlfriend will be arriving this evening, he reminds me, and so, although he'll be in town for a few more days, he won't really be able to spend more time with the likes of me. That message not delivered in so many words, of course, but clearly implied. And Rex being Rex, there has to be some gesture of summing up, some genial and ultimately condescending evaluation of my life. The Last Judgment of Hugh Norman, delivered by Rex Nairn, emissary of the ineffable. "Well, it's been good seeing you, after so long," he says. "You seem to have a good life here, I mean you're at home, this is your place." He seems to grope for something more positive to say, but then gives up. "Unfortunate that I didn't get a chance to meet, er, sorry, I've forgotten her name?"

"Maureen."

"Right. Maureen. Well. Sounds like you have a strong relationship. And you're obviously a significant contributor to the local cultural life." He hesitates. There should be a third item, but he can't think of one. I note with annoyance the slight stress on the word "local." He does stop short of saying "Well done."

It's clear that I'm not required to render a similar judgment on him.

And there's a brief coda, on Cliff. "Too bad about him. I've always thought he could've made more of himself. Even when we were kids. There was something stubborn about him, as though he didn't accept the world as it was, somehow. He'd go his own way, no matter what cost to him. Does that make sense?"

Yes. It does.

Friday afternoon, but at this time of year the student pub is almost deserted. Black Horse for Bill Duffett, Old Stock for me. I tell him about my discovery of the corpse of Leonard Churchill. But I leave out the connection to the character in the Karp story. I can't think of a way to make that fact either amusing or important enough to interest him. Why is that? He'd listen politely enough, looking puzzled, face slightly rearranged to accommodate an insincere smile. And I'd be embarrassed to have explained it. Too personal, too eccentric, beyond the bounds of our circumscribed area of friendship. Then we'd move on.

Duffett is relaxed, enjoying the realization that, given the way his interview with the committee has gone, he won't have to be Head of Department after all. But since this information isn't widely known, he's still being lobbied by colleagues with suggestions about how he would proceed if appointed.

"Craddock," he says, shaking his head.

"Craddock? Mr. Postscript? What does he want? Promotion to full professor? After what, two years is it?"

"No, he wants to change the name of the department.

"To what?"

"Writing in English and Popular Culture."

"Sounds like a winner."

"He's actually got the Dean interested, or so he said."

"The Dean."

"Let's not go there, Norman."

Duffett has still not forgiven the Dean—a recent appointment, a South Asian sociologist—for her comment, in her introductory address to the faculty, that, having grown up in the foothills of the Himalayas, she felt certain that she could handle St. John's weather, despite all the bad things she'd heard.

"So what's behind this? What's wrong with 'Department of English Language and Literature?'"

"Too restrictive, he says. And misleading. Nobody cares about language. People care less and less about specifically *English* literature. And pop culture is a crowd pleaser. Enrolment would explode. Or so he thinks. He wants to know if I'd be 'onside' with a move in that direction, more courses in, I don't know, things like the rhetoric of video games, the semiotics of the contemporary sitcom, that sort of thing. He himself is working on an article on something called *iCarly*. Ever heard of it?"

"No."

"Poor Craddock. I'm afraid Plover will disappoint him. He'll have a few choice words for her when she turns him down." This last comment is a reference to the fact that Craddock has become legendary among graduate students for his overuse of profanity in his seminars, a source of much amusement to them. Or so we've been told.

"Then there's O'Keefe. Wants a compulsory course for all English majors. To be called 'Imagination, Taste, and Judgment.' To make sure, she said that our students would be educated in the proper way of reading literature. She definitely used the word 'proper.' To counteract, how did she put it, 'our discipline's drift in the direction of...' Actually I've forgotten what it's in the direction of. Generally speaking, Lister Craddock, I think."

I have an image of Bernadette rising in a department, wielding a copy of, perhaps, *Beowulf* or *Paradise Lost*, imploring us not to discard our sacred traditions.

"Well, Alice will sort things out." I say this facetiously, as we both remember a department meeting when I noticed that while Alice Plover was in full mind-numbing content-free rhetorical flight, Duffett, sitting at a desk near mine, seemed to be taking detailed notes. When I cornered him later, he produced the sheet of paper on which he'd been writing. The "notes" consisted of a single short sentence, repeated dozens of times: "Shut the fuck up."

"Norman, I had to do it," he explained, "or there would have been mayhem." Such is the passion our discipline inspires.

And now he says simply, "Sure she will. Three more years of pointless infighting."

"Just like the last twenty or so."

We share a moment of silent low-intensity depression. The notion of a Duffett headship has been something I've thought would be a rare Good Thing, on the basis of integrity and well-intentioned-ness alone. On the other hand, it's certainly better for him not to do it. "I won't stay for another," I tell him.

"Another twenty?" He knows I mean beer. Or does he mean "stay" as in "stay alive?"

As if my life recently has not been sufficiently drenched in serendipity, as I'm driving home, half-listening to the radio, I hear Foley's name being pronounced. He's a "freelance theatre critic," according to the show's host.

"Last night," Foley begins, "the LSPU Hall became a parallel universe, the world of Aaron Spracklin's monodrama *A Man Alone in a Room*. And alone is what you feel as Spracklin gradually rolls out his scathing critique of late capitalism, for his character epitomizes the alienation of the individual in a society whose defining symbol is the pair of binoculars that provide the filter through which he interprets his experience. Binoculars seem to offer intimacy via the close-up view of their target. But it's a false intimacy, as the viewer is seduced into believing that the spatial gap between himself and what he sees is irrelevant. Spracklin's character, in the bitter isolation of his room, must learn this lesson, as the audience takes pleasure in observing the futility of his attempts to come to terms with the contradictions of his life. But when Spracklin turns his binoculars-enhanced visage toward the audience, that conglomeration of mostly well-heeled pillars of the community, you feel that the balance of power has shifted. Those who have paid the money that gives them the right to scrutinize condescendingly the performer's every word and gesture now find a very sardonic gaze being directed back at them. Or at least they should. And of course you must infer the sardonic nature of the gaze, since, ironically, because of the binoculars you can't see directly into Spracklin's eyes. Indeed, the binoculars act as a kind of barrier, protecting both Spracklin and his character, shutting down the possibility of perceiving him as anything other than an "artist" (consider that word to be enclosed in quotation marks) who sees the world through the lens of his own self-defined superiority. And so, although *A Man Alone in a Room* is on one level a searing indictment of capitalism, it is nonetheless itself a product for sale in the very marketplace that, logically, its author should seek to obliterate. You feel a pang of regret at this thought."

The emptiness of the house. The luxury of having all that space to myself, for once, even though there's nothing to be done with it. Frozen pizza for dinner. The excesses of last night catching up with me. The PBS *Newshour*. The Jays game. Who cares? I'm still mourning the Expos, two years gone now. No energy to read, let alone write. Banality, thy name is Norman's life. A man alone in a room. It occurs to me that I could use a good old-fashioned modernist epiphany about now, perhaps featuring, why not, the estimable Dr. Sherry Kirsch, whose dedication to family and to dental well-being could serve as metaphor for all that humanity has to throw in the face of death. Sherry hovering over me, probing gently with her shiny implements, icon of virtue and industry, labouring cheerfully to make the world a better place, the world figured as the microcosm of my mouth, that is.

But I won't be seeing her for another six months. As I ponder this fact, the ghost of Sylvester O'Connor, her suicided predecessor as custodian of my teeth, flits across the screen of my mind's eye, extolling the virtues of flossing.

The doorbell rings. Have I drifted off? I have no idea what time it is. The ball game is over, replaced by skateboarding highlights. It must be late. It must be Andy at the door. No one else would show up after midnight. Getting off the couch is a bit of a struggle.

The woman at the door is small, dark, and distressed. She doesn't speak English, either, and since my French is close to non-existent, our interaction is a comic amalgam of gestures and misunderstood or half-understood words or phrases, which, while no doubt providing an amusing spectacle for a hypothetical bystander, would be tedious to record.

It emerges that she's looking for Maureen. Maureen in her capacity as official of the francophone organization that she no longer works for. Someone, she can't explain who, has given her this address. Maureen is not here, I try to tell her. *Elle n'est pas ici.* She seems to understand, but the sense of urgency does not diminish. Somehow she has crossed the threshold—did I invite her to do that?—and shows no sign of leaving.

Is she being pursued? Is she in danger? Or simply deranged, on drugs perhaps? But she's managed to find her way here, and her speech, for all the emotion, seems purposeful, probably rational if only I could understand it. And her face, now that I look at it more carefully, seems somewhat familiar. I think of the sad-eyed woman on the poster that Maureen and I saw in St. Pierre, the poster that proclaimed her missing and, Maureen speculated, drowned. Can it be the same woman? Probably not. But I don't have the vocabulary to ask her.

But it's now clear what she wants. A place to stay. She desperately needs a place to stay. A safe place. I've figured it out. As it happens, I have room. Welcome. *Bienvenue.*

ACKNOWLEDGEMENTS

Thanks to my editor, James Langer.

Rebecca Rose, Rhonda Molloy, and all the folks at Breakwater.

Usual suspects: Libby Creelman, Ramona Dearing, Jack Eastwood, Mark Ferguson, Jessica Grant, Lisa Moore, Beth Ryan, and last but far from least, Claire Wilkshire, to whom I owe, well, pretty much everything.

 Larry Mathews is professor emeritus of Memorial University, where he taught in the English Department from 1984 until his retirement in 2015. He is the author of two previous books of fiction, *The Sandblasting Hall of Fame* and *The Artificial Newfoundlander*. He lives in St. John's with his wife, Claire Wilkshire. They have two children.